COMING OUT CATHOLIC

ALEX DUNKIN

COMING OUT CATHOLIC

ALEX DUNKIN

Buon-Cattivi Press

Adelaide, Australia

First published by Prizm Books, 2015
This edition published by the Buon-Cattivi Press, 2017
Adelaide, Australia

Copyright © Alex Dunkin, 2017
All rights reserved.

ISBN 978-0-9953661-2-1

Book design and cover art by Andrew Crooks
Printed by IngramSpark

This edition of *Coming Out Catholic* is dedicated to my family. Their endless support has made the milestones in my writing and personal life possible and worthwhile.

If Jesus Were A Gay Man

Jonathon and David
It was their time; strange, ancient, accepting.
Their memories gathered and stored inside Samuel's book,
at the ready for the faithful to latch hold.
Forever recorded; fighting, loving, dying.
Their friendship debated. Forgetting the high time in Samuel's books
shoving their faces through modern meanings. Seeking truth.
The Savior came: fighting, loving, dying
His love debated, similarity sought, his desires devoured.
Hasn't the world changed. What a farce.

CONTENTS

I.

IN SUMMER IT BEGINS

Here I am, on my knees in front of this man. Anyone would think that by sixteen (no matter how awkwardly I'm coming into manhood myself) this act would come naturally to me, but it doesn't. I'm a little bothered by this submissive pose, but I'm told submission is what makes the experience so powerful. My knees ache, my back grows stiff from the repetitive movement back and forth, my gaze fixed on the half-naked man I'm doing this for. I try to make eye contact, but his face is averted. I've always heard this is supposed to be amazing for me too, but I never feel it. All I feel is the hard wood under my knees. Seriously, have they never heard of carpet? There's not even a cushion. God, it hurts more now. When I have my own place one day, every room will be carpeted, no question about it. Lots of carpet and fine rugs to soften the place. No wood.

I'm over it now; I just want it to be done. I can't pull out now though, because people will talk. I know my reputation isn't great, and I can't afford for it to get worse. I keep rocking back and forth, hoping the ordeal will end soon. I can tell it won't be long now from the rising vocals—wordless, but still so full of meaning. I can feel the tension growing, feeling something rising up within. Wait for it. *Almost there.* I distract myself from the pain that penetrates my knees with the thought that it's nearly over. *Almost there…* At last, I ready my tongue to taste the life essence from the flesh of my Saviour in my mouth. I swallow it quickly, feeling guilty. The last echo dies from the room, 'Amen.'

Then it's my turn. 'Amen.'

Thank God, that's over. I hate communion at the best of times, and it's even worse at school. Sure, it's fun to mock and fool around with Father Donovan in religious ed classes, but his sermons leave a bad taste in my mouth. It doesn't make me want to purge my sins, just my breakfast. But I'm glad now that I can dust off my pants and wander back into class to daydream of a world outside my own, and usually about my classmates. Going to an all-boys school is all boys, most of my close friends are guys and I'm more comfortable with the thought of interacting with members of my own sex, but when I'm dreaming something else lingers in the back of my mind. Something strange and enticing tickles my imagination and hijacks my dream onto awkward yet exhilarating sexual encounters with guys from my class. I'm not sure if that's normal. I haven't spent much time around girls to see if they would venture into my daydreams just as naturally as guys do.

The proper teachers quickly usher us onto our next class. By 'proper', I mean they actually went to university and studied education to learn how to teach from some-one other than God. Not that I've turned apostate—I keep faith in His wisdom and His grace—but I can't bring myself to believe that a loving God intended his Word to be exactly like how the priests preach it. Until they iron out the crinkles in the fine print of the Bible I think I might listen to the actual biology teacher who knows about evolution, even though I'm not sure I understand it myself, but look how Mark's short blonde spikes always seem to be in the same place every day. And I'm happy to believe my physics teacher when he tells me about the Big Bang, although Mark's hair is always perfect, never a hair out of place. Then there are his striking blue eyes, bright to the point of glowing. And he always smells so good. He's like one of those plants my biology teacher was just talking about, that looks beautiful from a distance to lure in unsuspecting prey and then captures it as soon as it gets too close, digesting it slowly. What was I talking about before I got sidetracked… oh yeah. I'm going to hell. At least that's the deal according to the priestly teachings. And so maybe that's the best way to describe Mark, a beautiful trap and a hell of a best friend. The more time I spend with him the more my attraction to guys is confirmed, but I couldn't allow myself to fall into a trap that meant losing my friends, my family, my beliefs… my entire life.

I'm in the tenth grade now and these feelings have been growing (I like to think of it as blossoming) for quite some time. My feelings towards other guys, I mean. I think I like guys, and in a special kind of way. These feelings excite me, but they scare me more, and I don't think I can follow through with them. The faith I was raised with prevents me from even considering the possibility that I might like guys. How can I live a good Catholic life, and have a family and children, and be accepted into heaven if I like guys?

Most boys my age constantly think and talk just about sex, and in an all-boys college there's plenty of opportunity to share stories. I've heard some wonderfully graphic tales about their conquests, and about the girls who pandered to the every sexual desire of a few of the guys in my class. And while I'm vaguely aware most of it was boasting to cover how their first, three-second sexual encounter still blew their pubescent minds but still left them feeling inadequate, I'm honestly in no position to judge. I've never had sex, let alone good sex. I was even a late bloomer when it came to masturbation, going by the stories the other boys in my year level. I'm secretly ashamed that I don't have stories of my own to tell. I quite like the idea that they don't notice me as I mind my own business in class, ears pricked and ready to snatch a dirty secret whispered in the library or crowed in the change room.

'She got it all in. I couldn't believe it. I thought she was going to split in two!' Roger had once said. He was a mousy little guy with sharp eyes and a smooth smile. Back in the day—well a couple of years ago—that was the quote that started me masturbating, and led to so many complications. My mind flourished with the idea of Roger, little and lithe, six-pack gleaming with sweat, and a large, swinging cock throwing him off balance.

The idea threw me off balance too, and I headed for my bedroom. Caught up in my fantasy, I murmured 'Roger.' 'What?' Mum called back from the next room.

'What?' I returned, a little panicked. Embarrassment sucked the heat out of the room. I shook with chills.

'I thought you said something?'

'No, you must be hearing things.' *And I must be louder than I thought.*

'Okay,' she said and meandered back to whatever she was doing.

The stilted, awkward conversation did not perturb me at all, but merely slowed me down an extra ten minutes, five to get over the shock that I had called out Roger's name, and five to finish the job, so to speak.

Now that I think about it, it was around about the same time that the guilt started, a little terrier that snapped and yapped constantly in the back of my mind, refusing to give up the scent. It was a confusing time—it still is. I know I'm discovering sexual pleasure, but my mind always turns to guys, particularly the ones in class. I know it can't be right, though. I have to heed the teachings of Jesus, to live the life God intends for me, which means having a family. But how can I do that if I don't even think about having sex with girls? I've tried to. I've even prayed to be healed so that I can keep my faith. I love my faith. I draw so much strength from knowing God loves and provides for me, and forgives me along the way. The thought of having to give that up, or worse, having it taken from me, terrifies me. But I can't help the feelings pounding in my head, and everywhere I might turn for guidance—my parents, my friends, my teachers, my community—I'm told these feelings are some of the greatest sins known to man, an abomination.

But that's enough about me and my guilt—I'm a complex human being after all, and there's so much more to me than guilt. There's also embarrassment and humiliation, better known as physical education. The class—sixteen boys in all—marches out to the change rooms, gym bags in hand. The heat of the summer sun is fierce, but that's not why the sweat trickles through my shirt. It's not even that I'm crap at sport. I'm nervous about the change room, so much that it feels like the perspiration squirts out. I hate and love this part of the day. Fear tantalises me, curiosity teases down my spine. If I ever get caught looking at guys—y'know, perving— this is the place where it will happen, I'm sure of it. I'm careful to be subtle—my glances can flick around the room faster than a superhero can fly—but all it would take is one person to see me and I'm busted. I don't dare think about what would happen, the potential bashing, followed by bullying for life. I shudder. Sometimes I wonder if the person who catches my wandering eyes would be doing the same thing. Could someone else be looking at their classmates and pondering which one they like, or *like*-like or even just find attractive? Would they then hit on me? I've touched myself to these thoughts, fantasising that it was true, but then reality rushes back in and I feel alone again.

Mark charges in front of me as we reach the change room—he loves his sport. I envy his ability to mould into any game and come out on top, trophy in hand. I've never done that, and I couldn't even say why I wanted a shiny plastic cup to proclaim my victory. It'd sure beat the single tiny medallion for a team effort in basketball I was lucky enough to poach.

I sidle into the change room, almost as though I could hide under the smell of bathroom sanitiser and body odour that hangs in the air. I almost choke on it, or rather the excitement that rushes outward from my groin until it catches in my throat. Some of the class are already undressed. Boyish flesh of various shapes and sizes bobs around the room. I glance around quickly, pretending to be finding a place to dump my bag and begin the same process as the others. There is really no need to look— there's always space for me next to Mark. Everyone has their allotted place and nothing changes that.

The room is a fleshy array that exhibits the full range of the human body's possibilities. Scott wears his impressive mat of chest hair with a pride that defies his equally impressive rolls of flabby skin. He is twice the size of most boys in our grade, and three times the size of Tim, who strips off next to him, his lean muscles visible only due to his scrawny frame and dusted by fluffy pale hairs. Samuel swings his arms past his bare knees, aping a gorilla without actually attempting an impression. I can't make him out well as I glance up at his tall silhouette against the window. Sometimes I imagine him as an ogre so ugly the sunlight dares not show his true form. Other times I fancy him to be the dark stranger who'll whisk me away on a thrilling adventure, though that's a risk I'd never dare take.

I squeeze through the flab, folds and stench of the other boys to find my spot in the corner next to Mark. He's already in his shorts and has started on his shoes—he wastes no time in getting out onto the field. For Mark, time wasted changing is less time participating in the thrill of jogging. I don't think there is a sarcastic enough tone to emphasise how much he loves running. In my mind I've tried to pinpoint Mark's sexuality but I don't think he has one. Maybe sporto-sexual or something that involves pumping everything but yourself or anyone else. I'm sure that he and athletics will have a happy life together. They'd never argue or get sick of each other.

'Hurry up champ, you're going to miss the fun,' he says, slapping me on the shoulder.

'Alright, I'm getting there,' I mutter. He really is a great friend but sometimes, more often than not when sport is involved, he can be a little too full-on. But in reality I'm in no hurry. If I were to rush out of the change room with him now I'd miss out on the best part of perving: underwear spotting. I sometimes wonder if I might have a fetish for underwear. What a lovely way to describe it—*fetish*. It's a word I learned off the internet. Apparently having an interest that ventures into fantasies of a sexual nature is a fetish. I don't think there's much sexual content in the underwear in here, just pure amusement.

Some, like Randal, have spent all their money on nicer jocks 'for when I get a chick into bed' or so he would explain when bragging about his latest buy. I think it's more for when he pops into bed with his ego. Other than Randal, I don't think anyone else has puts much effort into the underwear they stow their essentials in, and there's only so much that mothers can do with sixteen-year-olds. They've probably given up trying to stop their teenage sons going out into the world wearing daggy, saggy jocks with cartoon prints on them. Or maybe it's a conspiracy among mothers, using unfashionably old jocks as contraception. Maybe they think we'll keep our childhood innocence so long as we have to hide our daggy underwear. But while the thunderbolt logo of the Mighty Morphin' Power Rangers might protect their teenage sons' virginity it won't protect them from ridicule, and no teenager should be burdened with that kind of shame.

One pair of underwear does catch my eye for more than just amusement. Instead of the usual daggy cartoon boxers, Thomas wears tight jocks that show off a signifi-cant outline. Cocks really are bizarre. I'm flushed with curiosity rather than arousal, fascinated by the shape. There is something completely unusual about it, even though I've seen one every day of my life. The variations you see for every other body part seem unremarkable, but the various shapes and sizes of cocks may as well be infinite, every one of them captivating, or at least this is what I've found through my exploration of the internet.

I stare at Thomas for far too long, much longer than I would usually allow myself. *That's interesting*, I think to myself as I look at the swelling bulge in his crotch, *perhaps not everyone here is a good Catholic boy.*

'What are you glaring at?' Mark startles me out of musing on penises with another friendly slap, this time on the butt. I snap back to reality with a sense of panic that I've been caught out, but Thomas had finished dressing while I daydreamed to leave me staring at a locker. I stammer an answer through my relief.

'Um… nothing.' A few seconds is all I need to assume a carefully crafted expression of indifference—I'd learned the hard way that innocence turns people suspicious, much better to hide behind a bored, uninterested face. 'I was just listening to Mac-C shouting.' Father McCormick has been shouting from outside for five minutes. As a phys ed teacher, the change room should be his domain, but teachers had been uncomfortable standing in a room full of half-naked boys since the inquests into institutionalised paedophilia.

'Well hurry up,' Mark urges. 'We've got baseball to get to.'

'Thrilling,' I roll my eyes theatrically, but I'm actually pretty pleased with today's activity. If it were cross country training again I wouldn't be as happy. Baseball is one of the lesser of the many, many evils of phys ed. I rush to lace up my shoes and follow Mark out of the change room at a jog.

* * *

'It's your turn to set up for dinner,' my older sister whines as she stalks from the kitchen, her long hair whipping my face on her way past. She's not even two years my senior, but to hear her bang on about her 'life experience' you'd think she had a good ten years on me. In reality this life experience amounts to a six-month experiment in goth make-up. To me she's just a wannabe rebel who swears, drinks, and complains like a twelve-year-old. I'm just happy she's the only sibling I have—I don't think I could handle two of her in the family.

Being a nuisance is nothing new for her, so I ignore it and wander onward, ready for dinner. I walk in on the usual scene of a weekday dinner, mum in the domain she claimed as her own—her kingdom of magical wonder— the kitchen, and dad at the table reading the newspaper from this morning even though he's no doubt already read the updated news online.

I set about preparing the table absentmindedly. My parents believe it's vital that we have a sense of purpose in the house, and for some reason think this can be achieved through chores. It's boring, but it could be worse. Once I'm done I carry plates of steaming vegetables and meat out to the table while mum zooms in on my sister to begin her daily child interrogation.

'So, how was your day, sweetie?'

'Fine mum,' Sarah snaps back, bristling.

Mum opts to ignore the attitude, 'Anything to report back from school?'

'No nothing mum, boring as ever.'

My sister and I share the dubious privilege of attending single-sex schools. She attends the girls school across town—it's a long way from us for a sister school. I guess that's what happens when there are only two Catholic schools in town. They put the boys at one end, girls at the other separated until the right moment.

'It's your final year, sweetie. I'm sure there's something happening to tell us? Any boys taking your fancy?' Mum chuckles merrily; my sister glares her in disgust. 'Ah, it's funny because you go to an all-girls school.' She gets nothing from my sister and me, not even a courtesy chuckle. 'Just joking, sugarlumps. Good thing you don't smile or you'd get crow's feet.'

'Wrinkles are just a sign that you've enjoyed life,' dad grumbles.

'I'm going to Katie's later. To study,' Sarah throws them a bone before any more attempts at humour can be put on the table.

Mum turns her crystal-sharp eyes towards new prey—me. 'And what about your day? Anything exciting happen?'

'Nothing much to report,' I say.

'How are your assignments coming along? Wasn't there something due for geography?'

'Yeah, it was about population and the makeup of families,' I mutter, repeating the monotonous information we were required to read several times in class.

'And … ?'

'And what?'

'What did you learn today?'

'Just that the way families are made up is changing. A decline in population growth, the nuclear family, and all that. Nothing too exciting. I was supposed to ask you and dad about your views on what makes up a family though. I should do that.'

'That's pretty simple,' dad pipes up. 'A mother and a father make a family.'

'What? Just the two of them?' I try to keep my tone light, but dad's words cut me, bringing home that one issue I tangle with constantly. Such a simple thoughtlessly conservative opinion really hits me hard. It hurts enough to think that I might never have a family. I couldn't even begin to discuss the reasons why that might be. Well, not with my parents, anyway.

'That's how it is, son. You can't have children without the mum and dad first. Other relationships can't have children and there's a reason for that.'

'What… what reason?' I mumble.

'It's just the way it is. Simple as that.'

'Oh,' I end the conversation by shoving a forkful of food in my mouth. I almost gag, but the action serves its purpose and cut the conversation short.

Mum begins her usual rant about how bad her job is and how her co-worker spends too much time shirking their duties or whatever. I focus my attention, other than trying not to vomit, on tuning out and choking down my mouthful while listing the reasons why I can't talk to my family about the turmoil going on in my head… about my sexuality.

I think I'm gay. There it is, out on the table. Well, not the table… just my own head, but that was hard enough. I don't find girls interesting, not in a sexual way anyway. They're a lot of fun to hang out with when I get the chance, but not much more than that. But other guys, they catch my attention all the time. But I'm Catholic, my parents are Catholic, I go to a Catholic school. Almost everyone I know is Catholic. And even though it can be stuffy sometimes, I love my faith. So I can't be gay. God just wouldn't let me be this way. And on top of that—the real kicker—I want to have kids, to have a family of my own, and to do that I have to be straight. Dad said it… it's as simple as that.

Confusion blurs the list of words behind my eyes in a swirling mass of reasons why I couldn't be gay. I tell myself that I will grow out of it, that I'm just interested in guys because guys are all I see—I'm surrounded by them at school.

After dinner I rush to clear my plate from the table and sneak off to my bedroom. In my small world I can pretend that everything is exactly how I want it and I can be happy in whatever way I feel. The words of denial haunt my steps to my bedroom, a leering mass of shadows waiting to crash down upon me in a single wave of destruction, but I don't have to deal with it when I'm in here.

I fall onto my queen-size bed, a hand-me-down from when my parents upgraded theirs, mattress flipped to hide their imprints so that all thoughts of my parents having sex are squashed to the bed frame. My scent on the quilt comforts me, warm and familiar. It knows me and I know it. I glare at the ceiling, where the fading outlines of glow-in-the-dark stars line the plaster. I've been in this room for too long. Stickers from my childhood still adorn my wardrobe. Marks on the wall show where posters once hung of the female pop star I pretended to have a crush on. My sister fuelled that 'addiction'. She had the entire magazine and assumed I would want the posters of a near naked celebrity. I did—it was good camouflage and stopped questions being asked. Now my disguise is nothing. If I show no interest in anything, no one will assume anything about what I like or dislike. I pray every night that this works, and I'm thankful in the morning that I get to hide for another day. Then at other times I ache to scream my secrets from the roof, but I could never face what would follow. I don't want to be an outcast for the rest of my life, without a family of my own. I want children, not just anyone's children but biological ones, my *own* children.

Across the room my tiny desk is piled with books. My Bible sits atop a pile of science textbooks. I know this is a strange juxtaposition, given that the followers of science and religion are uncomfortable with each other at best. It took me a long time to become comfortable with it myself. Eventually I realised that science and religion just answer different questions, the trick is just working out where to pose the question you want answered. I just wish I was able to reconcile my life (the real one) with the teachings of the Bible. They seem to be such enemies, battling to enforce their own position on each other just like I see happen on the news. Progress towards things like gay marriage seems to be happening, which I guess is good for me, but my heart aches at the thought of betraying my faith. Some days I would rather bleed than allow myself to break holy law. Obligations to fulfill His teachings consume me, just like our misgivings consumed Him. He died for the sins we continue to commit, and I can't describe the guilt I feel for a sin that seems to go to my very core. I cannot allow it. I have to repress any part of me that defies God's plan for me, or any clue that such a part of me exists.

Sometimes it feels really good to believe that my life is set up for me already, to know that there's a plan for me, a purpose. God knows what we are going to do, He should—He wrote the book on it. But how can I know what that plan is? Sometimes, when I forget myself (and let's face it, the world) in my room, the way I feel about other guys seems so natural, so perfect, that I know it's what He means for me. How could it be the wrong thing to do? And then that little priest on my shoulder (oh yeah, I don't get an angel and a devil, I just get a priest), he whispers, *but it could be a test*. What if my entire sexuality is just little hurdle God created to see how well I would overcome this difficulty in life. Dad would say it builds character—well, at least he would if it was *any other* test. And then the whole world comes crashing back in—my bedroom door doesn't always hold it out—demanding that I withhold my feelings, and bear up under this burden I've been given. But then I think of all the young guys (and girls) who proudly proclaim that they're gay—in high school!—and I think it's the bravest thing I've ever seen. And sure, they cop hell for it. But maybe that's the trial I'm supposed to live through, maybe that's the test. It scares me stupid to think that I might have to live through that hell too, and to have that torture done by my mates, my family, and my community. Jesus may have had the courage to go through that, but I don't think I do.

So, yes, I'm confused. My thoughts clash like this on a regular basis. Most of the time I concede defeat to the idea that I will be single and childless the rest of my life. It soothes my conscience to know that then I would only be lying to myself, it's only me that would have to suffer through it. At other times it's worse than that—sometimes it's the idea that I'll be married with the family that I want, and still be miserable. And miserable with me would be a wife and children, living with a pretender, a fake they shouldn't trust yet blindly do so. It's what I'm told (by the priests again, the big ones and the little one on my shoulder) is God's plan, but I know it would only be selfish. This I cannot allow either.

My mind shuts down for the evening. Too much thinking and processing causes my brain to go blank and switch off until everything cools down enough for a restart. I jump up and switch off the light. I can't be bothered with brushing my teeth, as it would mean leaving my bedroom and facing the reality of my family. It's just another reminder that I'm lying to people I love, and I don't want to feel like that right now. Maybe one day I can travel or something, where I'll get to be myself without hurting anyone back home. Not that I'll get the chance while I'm still at school. Until I graduate, I'll be stuck in a world where I'm tempted daily but allow myself to be bullied out of it by social expectations. It doesn't even know that it's picking on me. Damn society.

II.

AND SO THE WORK BEGINS

LEVITICUS 18:22—*cum masculo non commisceberis coitu femineo quia abominatio est*—I'm on my way to work as the old phrase tumbles through my head. Our religious ed teacher had drilled us with the translation—Thou shall not lie with mankind, as with womankind: it is abomination. Father Peter got pretty heated when he cited this verse as proof that gay sex is evil in the eyes of God, with little flecks of spit gathering in the corners of his mouth. Normally I'd laugh under my breath along with the rest of the class at Father Peter going over the top again, but this particular message concerned me, so I had just sat there thinking it over and praying for our usual religious ed teacher, Father Donovan, to return. I don't want to lie with a woman, definitely not in the same way that I'd want to lie with a man, so would that make it okay? Father Peter obviously didn't think so. Nor did the health teacher, when it came to the tiny amount of time from that class we spent on sex ed. I believe in the Bible, I really do, but sometimes it seems so unclear, and I don't understand how anyone can sound so certain when they claim to know what it means. One day I might understand, but for now I have a few hundred coffees to make and the chaos of a coffee shop to pretend to maintain.

'Hey,' Jenna calls from behind the coffee machine as I walk in. She's my boss.

'Hey,' I call back. 'Has it been busy?'

'Only just now. Straight to it.'

And straight to it I go. The usual onslaught of customers flood into the shop expecting me to know their names, and exactly what they want to order. There are a few I do actually remember—not their names, but their coffee orders. There are the *mega-hot-so-that-it-burns-anything-it-touches* flat white that I honestly don't know how he can drink. I even think it's illegal to sell coffee that hot thanks to an incident with a drive-through coffee and some old lady's crotch. She was probably beyond using her bits anyway so I don't know how she could sue for that. But I just give him his coffee at boiling point to avoid complaints. Then there's the *why-bother* coffee lady. She strides in, pants suit (what does she think this is, the 80s?), puffed out to perfect that powerful, masculine look. Some kind of 'if you can't beat 'em, join 'em' attitude, I guess. I might be just a kid, but my parents always taught me that hard work and skill is enough to get you the job of your dreams. Apparently, you can also do it with polish and bluster and shoulder pads.

'Very weak decaf soy latte?' I chime as she reaches the counter.

Jenna rolls her eyes. To a coffee fanatic this is a crime.

'That's the one,' the woman answers.

I wonder if she's heard of hot chocolate. You can still have the same cup we put the coffee in, but she'll actually be able to handle what's in it. Well, provided you put the marshmallow in the cup—leaving it on top is a big pink flag to coffee drinkers that will earn you a smirk of disapproval.

She moves along to wait the standard two minutes for her... *coffee*? I guess we still have to call it that.

'You're late,' Jenna barks as our co-worker sprints into the store.

'I know, the bus driver was a douche,' Daniel defends himself.

Daniel is my complete opposite. He's gay. Oh boy, is he gay. I've heard him tell Jenna stories of his nights out on the town, getting all excited about his sassy outfits. He wears his lisp and a limp wrist like badges of honour. For work he tones down the flamboyancy—well the clothes at least, not the attitude—so his fashion is now merely stylish. He still refuses to wear the new work shirts; the older, tight, tight shirts are much better at showing off his lean chest. I think he said he's a *twink*, which as far as I can tell means rather than working to get a hot body through exercise and eating well you just refuse to eat. Still, he does have nice abs. But then, whenever he's surprised, angry, excited, or has just come across some juicy gossip, his voice rises in pitch to a screech. There's nothing about him that I can relate to, and if this is what it means to be a gay man, I honestly don't think that I'm physically able to do it. I don't stand out, and I don't want to. I like being able to blend in, it feels safe. Fingers crossed this is where other guys like me are hiding: that they blend in so well that they aren't noted as gay, although it would be nice to know they are at least out there.

'Hey you,' he throws at me before joining me near the register to make people their food. 'My, my, it seems I got here just in time,' he adds, eyeing off the new arrivals to the store.

If there is ever a true collection of stereotypical football jocks, this would have to be it. Every one of them the same mass of lean muscle. Not so much that they look like they're about to collapse under the sheer weight of their bulk or turn on each other like a pack of wild apes, but just enough to show they run well and work out. I may have drooled a little, excited by the swaggering men entering the room, but also by the opportunity to stir some trouble with Daniel.

'Can I help you?' I jump in before Daniel has the chance to offer in his smooth flirtatious tone. I see his mouth gape out the corner of my eye.

Unlike with most customers, the pleasure in my smile as I serve these customers is unfeigned. It's definitely enough to make me forget about the Bible phrases that were haunting my thoughts only minutes ago. I have to be careful, though, to make sure I keep my eyes on the true prize—Daniel's frustration—and not get distracted by the hollow trophy of the rippling muscles under their light shirts. The lads all order, politely enough but entirely disinterested in the fact that Daniel's heart is shrivelling in a jealous rage. Jenna calls him to help on the coffee machine, and I swear his glare is practically lasers burning into my cheek before he flounces away. I smile and continue working, gloating on a small victory that no one will even know about.

It doesn't take long for the athletic guys to collect their drinks and disappear into the bowels of the shopping mall. That's the trouble with working in a food court, people are less likely to linger. I guess that's fortunate when dealing with customers such as Tofu Lady, a bulging blob of fat who eats only vegetables yet somehow manages to maintain an unhealthy sweater of lard. Other customers, ('guests', Jenna insists. Ha!) wouldn't be so hard to put up with if the hot ones would hang around a little longer to enjoy the scent of freshly ground coffee and be my eye candy. But they're gone too quickly, along with most of the other guests, leaving me to the onslaught of Daniel's ire. My only hope is to pretend not to know what all the fuss is about.

'You little cock,' he hisses, just quietly enough for Jenna and I to hear.

I don't know if his lisp is intentional or just what happens when you're truly gay. All the gay people I've seen (at least the ones on TV) have a lisp or speech impediment of some description. Could it be a sign of the gay? A permanent feature of the desire for men? But what would I know? Daniel is really the only gay person I've actually met. And spoken to, anyway. I've tried to meet others, online, but I was really shocked at how willing men are to push their greasy desires through the anonymity of the Internet. They were only interested in me if they thought

I'd get them off, and they weren't shy about telling me how in gruesome detail—it didn't make me feel good at all. In fact, Daniel was the only gay person who hadn't treated me like meat. Which meant I couldn't even tell him I was gay—what if he'd try it on me then too? And if Daniel is the most trustworthy person I know in the whole gay world, that doesn't paint a very good picture.

Especially now that Daniel is bearing down on me like an angry peacock.

'You're an arsehole, sometimes,' the bitching begins. 'You knew I wanted to serve them and you cut me off. I work my arse off and I should fucking get to look at the hot ones. I'm the better one at customer service, anyway.' His rant meanders into the back of my mind. I can't be bothered listening to the spiel about how life is unfair and me, me, me.

Compared to his usual fits of jealousy and rage, this was quite tame. His monologues are normally worthy of a dramatic role in a film, possibly a musical with the way his arms and legs flail about. In my mind the lights of the café dim while a spotlight shines on Daniel as he high kicks and pouts to the tunes of his idol: Kylie. Imagination has come to my rescue again, soothing the sting of Daniel's dummy spit as it converts the hissing of hate into a delightful image. This time it isn't even far from realistic.

Perhaps this is why Leviticus warns against being with another man—the drama is just unbearable. Maybe it's the sex that causes you constantly moving and squealing a newfound high note? I have wondered about the effects of anal intercourse but so far it hasn't been negative, not in my imagination anyway, which allows for the pleasure of intimacy to overtake any of the pain.

I snap out of my daydream to Daniel still ranting, but I'm not sure what about anymore. Something to do with a dog he lost when he was seven. Of course, Daniel losing a dog couldn't merely be a simple affair.

'He rocketed over the fence from the catapult we had been making. But we used too much glitter so we couldn't actually see him.' But then maybe he didn't say that, and I just dubbed in my own script to make it more amusing.

'Knock it off Daniel and get back to work,' Jenna barks surprisingly deeply for such a petite lady. I believe that could be the result of menthol cigarettes. They're as healthy as a piece of fruit, until inhaled.

The time at work crawls along, as usual. The low pay is just enough to add a few dollars to your wallet and warrant the return to work the next day. And before I know it I'm distracted again. This time my mind turns into swirling mush thinking about the world of employment I will have to navigate once I finish school. I'm confused about this too, and I don't even know what kind of work I'd like to do, or would be good at. Teaching is tempting, offering the chance to right any wrongs I've been dealt during my education. But by then I would have already spent thirteen years in school, who could be bothered with another forty? Perhaps I would like to get into something artistic. I don't mind art, except for the teacher. If only my father hadn't left such a memorable legacy with her class I would be able to pass through art unnoticed. Her wretched voice yaps at my heels as I try to express myself through the medium of creation. How can anyone concentrate with such a rigid instructor glaring down at them the entire time they're working? Not many people can, apparently, as her final year art class consists of only a couple of students. Personally, I doubt they're the best artists, just the more patient ones. It's the only way to get through her class.

'I need to duck to the toilet,' I inform Jenna suddenly. What I really need though is a break from my mind. She opens her mouth to protest and order me back to the counter, but I remove my apron and walk straight past in victory. No doubt she would argue that she deserves more time to do less, as she's the manager.

Daniel's glare is still icy as it follows my passage out of the café. He won't forget what happened until two minutes from now, when something more dramatic will distract him. He's easier to distract than jingling keys for a small child. And then I start to worry that all gay men will be like that. I want a partner who can maintain my attention for an extended period of time; otherwise maybe I'll just end up single and lonely.

I wander vaguely in the direction of the public toilets. There's no rush to get there, I just need to kill some time away from work. I've done it plenty of times, and never copped so much as a raised eyebrow. For some reason questioning someone's bathroom habits at work is off the cards for conversation, which is weird. It's not as if anyone is unfamiliar with what goes on there, and so for someone to take half an hour when they're supposed to be on the clock should set off alarm bells for everyone else. No one takes that long to do their business unless something isn't firing properly. I also think it's weird when people spend far too long in the bathroom without actually doing anything in there. Guys have a particular etiquette when it comes to using public facilities, which is mostly just get in and get out. Girls (according to my extensive knowledge acquired from movies) spend a lot of time comparing themselves, touching up minor flaws and gossiping in the bathrooms. Gossiping? Of all places I don't think that's the place for gossip, but I guess just like crapping, gossip needs to be done somewhere, and is probably best done where the rest of the world can't watch.

I reach the door of the men's, and suddenly the unspoken etiquette takes hold. The routine extends far beyond the actual pooping. The regular bathroom stench of piss and disinfectant wafts through the air as I open the door. My eyes instantly drop to avoid determining whether someone else might be in the room. This, I believe, is because toilet etiquette allows you to only be able to smell other people, not see them. In the event that eyes do unwillingly cross, a nod and a grunt is the most conversation allowed in any men's toilet situation. Violation of this rule would earn you the label of pervert, or worse… gay. They both seem to be lumped into the same category.

Perverts and gays, obviously only a perverted person would deviate from the sexual norm. There has to be something wrong with you to want gay sex.

And then, as always, insects start jumping around in my stomach as I approach the urinal, infecting me with jitters and internal itches. This doesn't seem normal, but I don't know because as I said, you don't talk about what happens here. My skin prickles, forcing hairs to stretch beyond their limits, seeking to detach themselves from my body. They too feel the shame that is encroaching on my thoughts. My heart tries to make good its escape from my chest, and the sense of danger grows: I have to expose myself, when someone might walk in at any moment and see. My breathing stops and I risk a look around the room, eyes ready to drop should they see another man. I only break the code of conduct because I need to find myself a cubical. My darting eyes quickly become a full turn of the head in my hunt for total privacy. I know other people must be in the room; I sense their presence.

There! In the corner I spot it. One free cubical. I shoot across the tiles and bolt the door behind me. Every muscle within me eases back into the natural flow of necessities. Without this thin veneer of privacy I would be stuck, unable to relieve myself. As I let go I relax, but also hang my head in disgrace: I am pee shy.

I still remember exactly when this issue took hold of my life and claimed my confidence in the bathroom. The images of that day come back to me now. A school trip, five years prior. A suddenly onslaught of tourists and students disgorge from two buses at a small town rest stop, overwhelming the only available toilet block. Pressure built inside my bladder, but also inside my head as I falter at the last moment. My cock was out, ready to extinguish the invisible fire in the toilet, but the water supply clogged by anxiety. Since then it hasn't been the same. And now I'm stuck in the cubicle, peeing like a girl.

I take as long as possible, enjoying the forbidden third shake. I'm definitely playing with my cock, but it's for a worthy cause, the avoidance of work. I instinctively look over my shoulder, but only God is watching me now. I take the fourth shake and replace everything inside of my pants with a hint of pleasure gleaming in a quick smile—it doesn't take much touching myself to forget my problems.

Solemnly I return to the work at hand. It's only for five hours at a time but still, making coffee for so long exhausts my imagination and overstimulates my senses. The constant waft of caffeine is enough to keep the nose hairs alive and raving until dawn, which will hopefully be long enough to finish my homework and get ready for the constantly nagging requirements of school.

III.

TOGETHER WE PRAY

A CHILL in the air heralds the dangerous months ahead. Not literally dangerous. I mean, it's not likely to sneak up behind you and clobber you with a bat while you're occupied with your shopping. But when we receive the first taste of autumn it's as if it immediately begins to swallow up the warmer air. It feels as if the year is well and truly swinging past. It won't be long before the shivering misery called 'winter' will crush down on our chests. This might all sound a little melodramatic, but it's just a smidgen of exactly how much I dislike the winter months. It's too cold to spend time outside, and so dark I feel like a stalker when I creep between home, school and work.

As usual, when the cold weather hits Father Donovan starts to look like one of these suspicious stalkers, until you meet up close to him. His attire is awkwardly creepy yet the warmth in his smile and his unwillingness to share the potentially flu ridden breathing space occupied by students is generally enough to dismiss the idea that he's an actual creep. At the first whisper of cool air he layers himself in the thickest, brown jacket ever invented and buries himself in the warmth of a thousand scarves. He looks like a mushroom on steroids, bulging in all the wrong places. I have to hand it to him though, I've never seen him sick and possibly this is why.

Father Donovan glides into the room and peels off the layers of winter clothing. As usual, I'm sitting next to Mark on one of the pews. For our religious education class, we're both really excited to visit (wait for it) the school chapel. It's not for anything special, just confession. With the change of seasons comes the change of mentality. Summer is when all the fun is to be had, and now that the trap of winter clenches tighter we must submit to the suffering and repenting. Father Donovan takes his seat at the front of chapel, just out of normal hearing range of all the students.

'Who's up first?' he shouts over his shoulder. Predictably, no one moves upon this first prompting. 'Right Randal, you're it, I imagine you'll have a lot to get through.'

Snickers fill the hollow room. Father Donovan is right; Randal has always had a lot to share with the kindly old priest. Three years ago I remember him crying on his way out. I guess it could have been because he blamed himself for his parents' divorce, or because he'd been mocked in the change room for his smaller than average cock. The way he talks about it you wouldn't think it was so small, but how would I know? I wasn't the one to whip out the measuring tape.

'Why must we do this so often?' Mark questions, not for the first time.

I have a selection of standard answers, all of which have been used in the past. *It gives us a chance to work on our creative skills*—or—*It's the only time we can bitch about our teachers and be forgiven no matter how much we swear.*

'Because this is a good Catholic school and like all good Catholic boys we have to feel guilty,' I would have chosen a gentler answer but I'm feeling snarky in this cold weather.

'Yeah, but this much?' Mark complains. 'I start to feel bad when I don't have anything to say. Last time I made up a sin and now I have to confess the lie.'

'Well lucky you did that otherwise you'd have nothing else to talk about again.'

'What's that supposed to mean?'

'You know.'

'No not really,' Mark gazes at me with an expression of innocence glistening in his eyes. Sometimes I wonder if he does anything wrong, that might ever be seen as sinful or even malicious. Possibly on the football field he might get a little aggressive, but even then I've seen him help opposition players up after he's knocked them down, and once he even stopped to give one of the younger players a pat on the back, a word of advice and then hand over the football instead of taking off for a goal himself. He's just so good and perfect in everything that he does.

'I just don't think you're a nasty person,' I explain. 'I've never seen you do anything that would constitute a sin.'

'What do you mean by that?'

This time I'm the one to give a blank look but he quickly matches my empty stare. 'It means I don't think you are a bad person in anyway,' I reply.

'Oh. Well, you don't need to be a nasty person to sin.'

'Faggots!' A hideous, out of tune voice interrupts our

conversation. I don't have to turn to know its Chris, the school bully's bully. 'Looking into each other's eyes like that. You love him don't you, faggot.'

It isn't the first time Chris has used such words used against me. Normally they don't get as inventive as 'faggot'. 'Gay' usually maxes out his creativity. He must have discovered a new word, and now intends to get maximum mileage. The problem with Chris, well the main one, is he can't read the signals people give off. He doesn't know when to back off and doesn't like to lose. It's a pity—he'd be pretty attractive is he wasn't such an arsehole. With him it's true about beauty being on the inside, his is a steaming mess of shit oozing out of the bowels of a diseased earthworm. And that's on a good day.

'Rack off, Chris,' Mark stands up for both of us.

'Rack off,' Chris mocks. 'I don't have to do what an arse-fucker says.'

'Good, you can do what I say then.'

Chris is slow to respond, overcome by this intellectual maneuvering. I begin to cower within myself. I don't like confrontation and I don't like the exposure. The wrong message might be snatched out of the air by anyone within earshot if I give the faintest sign that I actually am what Chris says. Chris arches his back as he prepares for a real fight. Mark though, is bored by the imitation of masculinity. Mark isn't violent, but he is powerful when he needs to be. Mark stands, slowly unwinding the full extent of his height. The extension of his limbs threatens to never end. Chris feebly attempts to arch up even more, but the broadness of his shoulders is nothing compared to Mark's sheer bulk. There's fierceness in Chris' animal rage, but it's outmatched by the skill of a pure athlete like Mark.

Father Donovan swoops in on our confrontation. 'Right, you're next,' he orders, glaring straight at me, his eyes burning into mine as though he could read the truths of my life. 'Well come on, let's get this thing started.'

I jump out of my seat and begin the march to the front of the chapel.

'Faggot,' I hear the final snipe from Chris.

I sense the commotion settling down behind me. Father Donovan seems uninterested in the fight that had the potential to break out. He didn't even question what was happening. I start to think he was only there as a matter of good timing. I walk past Randal, who's looking slightly pale but not really worse for wear.

'Right. Sit,' Father Donovan gently commands. Kindness and forwardness, an unusual combination of interpersonal technique that only a man like Father Donovan could ever master. 'Now, take it from the top,' he starts in an almost knowing fashion, he knows how to get through to teenage boys. I guess he was one once so would know exactly how it feels for us to be teenagers now.

'Um,' I present my usual thoughtful stutter. 'I'm not sure where to begin.'

'You know,' Father Donovan leans back in the front row pew. 'We've been through this process before. This is a time of cleansing and reflection. You are not judged in the eyes of the Lord. You are always acknowledged and forgiven.'

'Pfft,' I roll my eyes.

'Yes, always forgiven,' Father Donovan presses on. 'I'm going to tell you the same thing as I did your friend over there,' he nods in the direction of Randal.

'I don't think "friend" is the right word for how we get along.'

'Doesn't matter, you must all get along eventually. How many people you think you've conquered or how many *chicks you have banged* doesn't account for much in the eyes of our Lord. How you love others is what's important and as long as you have that I know that God has a place in his heart for you. After all, he has a place for everyone, especially those who do good deeds for others.'

My mind is still reeling from a man of the cloth somehow managing to say 'chicks you have banged'. I think I may have underestimated Father Donovan. He appears to be knowing in the ways of the youth.

'Not all priests are as old fashioned and ignorant of the world around them as you might believe,' Father Donovan continues. 'I'll have you know that I've experienced more in today's world than you, young pup. That's part of my job, to understand what's going on in the world and to guide people on the path of our Lord, but only when they are willing. You can't force this stuff, you know. A lot of people, particularly you boys here, don't like to be told what to do, especially when it comes from what I heard one of the older students call '*somebody else's imaginary friend".* This priest is starting to blow my mind with quotes. 'Okay, so this is the perfect time to spill something that you've been holding onto, so you can understand someone else's opinion on it without judgement. You don't have to take immediately to the Lord and ask for forgiveness, but I'm definitely the right person to talk to if you want to.'

'I'm sorry Father, I didn't mean to be dismissive,' I reply. 'I guess I'm just a bit shaken up by what just happened with Chris.'

'And why is that, my boy?'

Father Donovan's smile warms the room. I uncurl slightly from my protective hunch to match his daring eyes. From past experience, I know Father Donovan would never pass on a word of what people confess, and he had never held the confessions within hearing range of the others in the room. He has a knack for privacy, this man. I look again at the honesty on his face. *What the hell,* I think. I take a breath.

'I think I'm gay,' I whisper.

I shut my eyes. My breath ceases while my heart races. I await the wrath of God to strike me where I sit, but it does not come. No earthquakes. I do not spontaneously combust. I'm still here, perched in an ugly cower while Father Donovan continues to look upon me with the same honesty as before. He is not shocked by my statement. He inhales slowly, knowing exactly how to move to prevent me standing up and screaming like a lunatic who thinks his Transformers are raping his Barbie doll (I saw this happen at the mall once during work—it wasn't a fun day). His exhale smoothes the ripples in the air.

'That was an extremely brave thing for you to say. Can I ask why you have chosen to?'

'Um, because it's true, it is what I think. I guess it would be a good time to air out all the issues in my life, and I listened to what you said about getting another perspective. I've been denying it completely for a long time and now, I'm openly admitting it to someone. I guess I'm saying it now just so I can confirm it to myself. Not really confirm it but now that I've said it, it feels real, it feels right. I can't be sure, I guess. I haven't been with a guy, or a girl for that matter. But all my feelings lead me to want a relationship with a man. I hope that speaking up about it now might get me well and truly in line for forgiveness later on when I actually need forgiving, for sodomy or something like that. Not that I would be into sodomy, but that's what two guys do together isn't it? It feels so natural for me though, so it can't be against God's will, can it? He must have already decided for us that is would be this way. Or is it just a test? I get so confused about it all. How can I be sure that I really feel this way? I'm not sure about anything anymore. I mean, I want kids, I really want a family but how am I supposed to have kids if I'm in a relationship with another man?' I pause to catch my breath. I don't know how that happened but Father Donovan, only by an honest glance, sucked out so much of my identity and my confused thoughts in one hit. He had just waited in silence throughout my whole litany. My layers of camouflage were useless against the understanding on offer. I wait again, pausing in dread at the potential responses. How is a priest supposed to react to that? Slapping the gay out of me is the first thing that jumps to mind, followed by a gentle beating with the Bible and a good splash of Holy water just to make sure. I wait, I fear. I am wrong.

'Let's take it from the top,' he begins gently, offering no sign of condemnation. 'Thank you for opening up this part of your soul to me. It's not something that just anyone your age can admit to willingly. To your questions about God and sodomy, as you said it's something that you don't know about yet, but for future reference God destroyed the city of Sodom due to acts of idolatry and rape, not sodomy as is so commonly believed. And besides, He was a wrathful God then but He's much more into forgiveness now. And while God may send us many challenges, there are no tests. It's just life. We live it as naturally as we can and God will always forgive us for any mistakes we might make along the way. To love is the Godliest act any of us can achieve, and there's no wrong way to do it.

'And to your final point, a family. You should know that a family comes in all shapes and sizes, particularly in today's world. You can see that just in the number of students here with divorced parents, and most of them are Catholic. Can I just reaffirm, you have done a very brave thing sharing your feelings about your sexuality, particularly at school. You must follow you heart; it's the only thing that knows what's right for you. Now, off you go, I've got half an hour left and I've only seen two of you. I hope this has helped you. Like always, feel free to hunt me down if you need to talk. It's my job. Now off to study.' Father Donovan turns his head over his shoulder. 'Next,' he shouts. 'Looks like it's you, Mark.'

I'm still flabbergasted by Father Donovan's remarks as I walk past Mark. Mark grunts some form of acknowledgement at me, or it could have been a question, I'm not entirely sure. I'm too caught up in Father Donovan's response. Everyone in the school knows he's a bit of a dark horse, or a rebel within the priesthood, but I never expected him to be so lenient on this matter. But it had certainly planted a seed of reassurance within me. After all, he said it can't be wrong if I'm following my heart. While there are still excerpts from the Bible that seem to be against gay relations niggling away in the back of my mind, I'm not so sure of them now. I float out of the building and into the open air. I don't notice any of my peers sitting around waiting for their turn to confess.

If I was actually paying attention to anything happening outside my own thoughts I would've noticed the fist flying at my face. Pale knuckles charge angrily towards my cheek. I feel an instant sting slice through to the other side of my head. A splitting sensation rushes through my skull. The bone feels like it's shattering. My mind blurs. I can't decide between yelping at the pain, collapsing into a blubbering mess, or sheltering myself from a potential onslaught of blows. I don't get to make any decision at all though as I'm pushed back against a wall by the force of the blow, and I begin to slide down it as my feet give out from under me. Luckily for me it's just the one punch.

'Fucking faggot,' Chris spits on me. His warm saliva oozes down my inflamed cheek. I've never loathed someone so much as I do at this moment. 'Did you enjoy telling the pedo about how much you like getting fucked up the arse?' He isn't subtle about his insults, he goes right for the throat with the crudest words he can think of, and I doubt he really knows his insults hit so close to home. 'You did, didn't you, you sick prick. If you ever try anything on me, I'll fucking kill you.' He spits again, this time marking his territory on my sweater. Triumphant, he walks away, back into the chapel.

Insult and injury are not pleasant feelings. But worse yet, I feel humiliated. My pride has been smashed and pummeled into dust to blow away on the next wind. I huddle into myself and wonder why no one comes to help me. I soon realise everyone else is still in class except for two younger kids at the end of the hall looking over their shoulder as they flee the scene of the crime. They must have seen what happened but are scared out of doing anything. I would have to nurse my own wounds for the time being. I haul my weary self up onto unstable legs. The ground seems to shake, but it's just my legs wobbling under the unwanted weight of my body as I begin the slog towards the bathrooms. Voices echo in the halls along the way. Their giggling fills me with hopelessness.

I know they are near but I have no faith that they'll help me either. I hobble faster, my feet as uncertain as if it were my legs that copped the beating.

The hundred metres from the chapel to the toilet block suddenly appears a vast, impossible-to-cross space. My mind swims in the shock and adrenaline. This is a new experience for me, being beaten up by a bully. The worst Chris could usually do was a couple of unintelligent words that his dad taught him the night before. The dumb words still hurt, and it usually takes me a while to find any sense of my self-respect again afterwards, but the physical assault is a different level again. It's really shaken my world—how can I ever expect to feel safe again when such an unexpected, unprovoked attack could come from anywhere, at any time. Suddenly I'm overwhelmed by a sense of shame. Shame of who I am, shame that I couldn't protect myself, shame that maybe I deserved to be bashed because of the sickness in my soul. It feels so shameful that I can't even bear to tell anyone about what happened, not even those closest to me.

My head spins messily as I stagger into the toilets and over to the basin. Heat swarms in my mouth as the blood gushes freely. Outside, I can feel a bruise coaxed from within my skin. I look into the mirror, prepared for the worst, but I soon see that it's my ego that's been bruised far greater than anything else. It certainly feels like there should be more to show on my face than the disappointment in my eyes. I press lightly on my cheek. The sting is instantaneous, but no bruise seems to want to emerge. In a way, I'm glad. I don't have to report Chris to the office (or my parents) and make myself out to be some kind of snitch, which could only lead to far worse consequences.

Time floats on somewhere behind me, freely dancing away with the breeze. I don't notice the lesson has passed until I hear the howls of a mass of students moving around the corridors. I snap myself out of my daze, splash water to clean off the spit from my cheek and my jumper, and sulk off to the next lesson I'm supposed to attend. My body will be present for history, but I doubt my brain will be up for learning anything.

'Where've you been?' Mark greets me as I sit at my desk.

'Wagging,' I mumble, trying to retain some of my pride.

'Mate, that's not like you,' the concern in Mark's voice stings almost as much as my cheek.

'Just drop it,' I say as gruffly as I can muster, though it's probably more the pleading in my eyes that gets the message through.

Mark shrugs. He usually doesn't ask too much detail, but he knows all he has to do to get me to talk is sit tight until we leave school and the social requirement to lie dries up. But within these grounds, I need to maintain some shred of cred (as they call it) if I'm to survive high school alive, and enjoy the freedom that I hope to find in university.

IV.

WHEN THE LYING BEGINS

It isn't exactly my style for a night out, but Mark convinced me to come along to this party hosted by a buddy of his from one of the sporting leagues he happens to belong to. I don't know which—I can never keep up with any of the sports teams Mark talks about. Whenever conversations become a little sports-heavy I keep nodding and grunting at the right (I guess?) moments to show my approval of whoever is sharing their athletic prowess. When it's just us two hanging out Mark usually tones down the sport, although occasionally he can't stop himself and he'll rave enthusiastically and in great detail about his hopes for his sporting future. I just let him go for it and continue with the video game at hand. Mark stops talking eventually when he realises I'm several levels ahead of him.

Throughout this party and its many conversations I tightly clutch a warm beer and feign sips to keep up the look of the thing. Mark and his sport fiend friends guzzle it like water (or coffee), but I can't bring myself to do more than bring it to my lips—it tastes vile. I wonder if the entire attraction to beer is that they think drinking the manliest manly man's drink adds to their appearance of machismo. To be short—I hate beer. I'm sure it was more of a discovery than a creation, like someone falling face first into a chilled puddle of deer piss.

We're not there long before Mark abandons me. Well, physically I'm the one to wander off, bored with the topic of conversation, but Mark dragged me here practically against my will, and so it's his job to make sure I'm entertained. I decide to sit in the corner on a couch and watch the skills on display from the other partygoers. From what I can see, I'm glad I'm not expected to participate in their games. The sumo wannabes jiggling their rolls of skin in front of me and slamming their bellies together are a delightful sight. There always has to be a few in the sports team that don't fit the athletic body type. Party-watching is similar to watching small children play a game of tag. One of them runs around tapping others on the shoulder, upon which they are required to hoist the contents of their hands into the air and throw back as much of the alcohol as they possibly can. Once they've proven their worth they can choose the next person to consume the maximum amount of booze in the shortest time. The only real difference between the partygoers and children is that children stop when they're tired and cranky, whilst these guys stop when they're tired and in a coma. Not even vomiting always holds them back. Charming imagery, I can assure anyone. Some of the guys here are pretty hot, with their athletic bodies and all, although as they soon start to get really messy, I'd be glad to have my own vision obscured under a haze of alcohol.

This party wouldn't be so bad if I knew more people here. Mark is the only one I know, and he's off talking stats of some description with a group of guys outside. A couple of the more friendly jocks had approached and tried to talk to me, and I tried to care about the number of runs the local champs had managed that day, but quickly the fact that I don't care *at all* creeps in and kills the conversation. So I'm inevitably lured into the kitchen to wait for the time when the stumbling drunks get into exploits worth reporting to the gossip channels at school. A first-class house party has three defining features: a car crash, sex of some kind, and a fight. These three ingredients will fuel the fires of gossip for weeks to come, and just being at that party, even if it's only momentarily, will put you on the social map. I just hope they happen tonight so that it will be worth my while coming here.

I take an absentminded sip of my beer and regret the motion immediately. Damn habits. When a drink is in your hand, you do exactly that, drink. A body glides past me to take a seat on the neighbouring countertop. A rosy fragrance arouses me out of my self-pity.

'You're too cute to be sitting by yourself,' remarks a charming voice. 'I'm Sandra,' she offers her hand. I take it and introduce myself. 'Nice to meet you. So who here dragged you along and dumped you?'

'That would be Mark, the tall guy outside.'

'They're all tall outside,' she giggles.

'The Mark that knows everyone here from playing every sport imaginable.'

'Oh, that Mark. I know him. He's hot. I think he broke up a fight outside just before.'

She's right, Mark is hot. I want to tell Sandra that I agree, but I hold my tongue. She's quite cute herself. A peachy gloss warms pouting lips, framed by glowing bronze curls that dangle past bare shoulders. Her curves are full like her lips, their perkiness effortlessly supporting the black dress in all the right places. My mind races and twists in all sorts of confusing loops. I can see that she's attractive—that part's not confusing, I've always been able to appreciate the beauty in a woman's figure. What's confusing is that I'm attracted to her, and that doesn't happen. I sit there in stunned silence for a moment just trying to process this information. Maybe I'm not really gay, maybe it was just a phase, maybe God has answered my prayers and made me better, and maybe I really just hadn't met the right girl yet. Gah! It's all so confusing.

Sandra isn't ruffled by my lapse into silence, and pushes on with the conversation.

'So, which school?' She is direct, but with a smile in her voice, and on her lips—I decide I like it. I tell her my school, and her eyes light up. 'Ah, our elusive sister school. How's that working out? I can't decide if I find it harder being surrounded by girls, or being surrounded by Catholics.'

'I don't really know any different,' I tell her. 'I've been going to the same school most of my life. The only girl I know is my sister, and I hope they're not all like her. But whatever. You're not Catholic?'

'I am according to my parents, but it's not really working out for me. And don't worry, most girls are probably worse than your sister when you cram them all into one school together, but a few of them are awesome, like me.' She grins. My sister would sound so full of herself saying something like that, but Sandra makes it sound confident and fun and, well, cool. 'I get what you mean though. My dad is the only guy I see during the week, and even then he's too tired to talk, or really care. Mum keeps him up to date with our goings on, I guess.'

The self-assurance drains from Sandra's face for a moment as she speaks about her father, and I think about mine, and how it's my fault that some distance has grown between us. All the while I've been trying to cover the issue of my sexuality, have I been blocking any potential connection with my father? I quickly try to change the topic. 'Yeah, well my sister is one of those girls at your school, so maybe that's where she gets it from. What happened to all your friends tonight? You got dragged along and dumped as well?'

'Pretty much. That's Stacey over there swinging off her boyfriend pretending to give a rat's arse about sport.'

'Why does she bother? I tried it for a while for Mark's sake, but I just couldn't keep it up.'

'I know right. No one should be that interested in sport. And her dumb-arse boyfriend should know better than to try and make her care about his tackle record. I mean, come on. A heap of guys in short shorts, touching each other up. Kinda gay, don't you think?'

There's the key word: 'gay'. Sandra just throws it out there so easily, so mindlessly, but it hits me for a six. It slashes my self-confidence of course, but more than that, it's *confusing*. I find sports, especially football, so manly it's intimidating—even the bit where they pat each other on the butt. And here's this incredibly hot girl, poised calmly calling it gay. Does that make not caring about sport the straight thing to do? My internal monologue has no chance to get carried away though, Sandra keeps the ball rolling.

'I tried to be interested,' she continues. 'But it's obvious I just don't care.'

'I couldn't agree more. They recount a match like it's an old war story, full of sacrifice and glory. But I don't get it. Congratulations meathead, you kicked a bit of leather from one end of a field to the other. But has it cured cancer? Maybe if they grunt at it enough, their manliness will scare it away.'

Sandra laughs. 'That's a little harsh.' Her laugh is sweet and merry, and gives me a tight little shiver of delight that she laughed for me. Still, I try to defend my position.

'No, it's about spot on. Anyone would think from their attitude that the fate of the world is held in the balance. They scream as though they've saved the earth from certain destruction when they win a game by a point, but it really hasn't accomplished much. And when they lose it's a tragedy beyond compare, but they don't recognise that they'll get to do the same thing all over again next week. And then it's finals season, which is even worse.'

'So much testosterone, so few brain cells.'

'Yeah and when all you've got is testosterone but no

brain cells to direct it, then I guess a barrage of tackles and head butts are all that's left to you. Unfortunately, I feel I've been cursed with both—testosterone and a broader perception beyond the sports field, that is.'

As we both laugh, Sandra drops a hand on my leg. Physical contact—a nerve fires off down into my crotch. The automatic response awakens my dormant cock. I'm a little off-put that it's been triggered by a girl, but no one has touched me like that before. The spark calms quickly, and confusion rises in its place. I can't be sure if it was an automatic response or a true one, or if the automatic response is the true one. 'I take it you don't play any sports,' Sandra interrupts my train of thought before I get carried away again.

'I did when I was younger but nothing now. I lost interest when it stopped being a social sport and suddenly became competitive—it wasn't fun anymore.'

'So you're here out of moral support as well?'

'I think so. Or it could just be that I'm a pity case. Mark's a good mate and he makes me go out and socialise and stuff, but he gets distracted easily, y'know by seeing a rival or food, or something like that. At least he stopped to get me a drink on the way through.' I hoist my beer and throw it back like I've got something to prove. I've nursed it so long that it's grown warm and I almost retch. Sandra hurls her head back in a fit of giggles—mirthful without being mocking in a way that soothes my embarrassment.

'I don't think you enjoyed that too much,' she gets

out through her giggles. 'Look, you don't have to pretend around me.'

I freeze. Pretending? She doesn't know anything about me, how can she see through my mask so quickly? 'You don't like beer,' she elaborates, and I hold back a sigh of relief. 'I'm not a fan of the stuff either.'

'That's what was on offer. It isn't sweet enough for me. It's weird; I love my coffee bitter but when it comes to cold drinks it has to be sweet.'

'Snap. Stacey thinks it's weird that I won't have sugar in my coffee, but I gag if it's too sweet.'

'I know. I think I'm only drinking this because it's in my hand, and I have no idea what else there is on offer.'

'Pretty much nothing.' Sandra pauses momentarily. A sly grin creeps between her cheeks. 'I know where we could get something a little sweeter. Come with me.' She snatches my hand as she leaps down from the bench. I almost lose an arm as she drags me between the wrestling brutes and puking 'rebels'. Sandra leads us directly to the stairs and straight up to the second level.

'You know your way around,' I observe.

'Yeah, I've been here with Stacey, it's her ex-boy-friend's house.'

'Wait, what?'

'She's made her way through a few sports teams. I love her, I really do, but she dates athletes just so she can sleep with them.'

'So she's a bit of a slut?' I cough out without thinking, then cringe as I hear what I've just said.

'Dude, you can't shit-talk my friend like that unless you want a slap upside the head. Especially that word—it shames girls who enjoy sex, while guys who sleep around are celebrated as studs.' Then she grins again. 'Besides, shit-talking Stacey is my job. I guess she sleeps around a bit, but not really. She's always in a relationship when she sleeps with a guy, so she's more of a serial monogamist.'

'Interesting concept. Sorry for being a douche.'

'Nah, don't sweat it,' Sandra assures me as she throws open the doors into a bedroom. I exhale loudly as I gape in awe at the size of the room. I think we have stepped into another world—the master bedroom must be larger than my entire house. Plush rugs and faux furs adorn every surface of the room in layers of gold and deep browns.

'If you think this is nice, you should see the en suite.'

'There's more?' The awe in my voice while I gawk around is almost embarrassing, as I realise just how much mum and dad must scrape by just to send me to that school.

'Yeah, it's more like a hotel,' she says, opening the door into another realm beyond the bedroom. She isn't wrong—the en suite is a palace. The bathtub forms a centerpiece surrounded by glistening tiles and accented by a small fernery built into the end of the room.

'I didn't know this place was so swish. Why would they let a party happen here?'

'Because not many people know how much they've spent on these rooms. The rest of the house is pretty standard, but from what Stacey says her ex's parents wanted a retreat within their own home, so this is what they did. Plus, I bet they're away for the weekend and don't know about the party at all. This way, I'll show you the little secret we're here for.'

She heads over to an impressive television cabinet at the other end of the bedroom and opens the oak door to reveal a mini-fridge. A tinkling signals the delightful array of sweet alcohol contained inside. I snatch a glance at the variety of colours in the fridge; I instantly recognise whiskey, gin, tequila, and vodka. For a good Catholic boy, it's surprising how much I know about alcohol. Well, other than communion wine, of course.

Sandra works her magic on the little baby bottles of booze, pulling out vodka, cranberry juice and a couple of chilled glasses. In the same movement her spare hand dashes out to find the ice hidden in the small freezer. And the whole time her pose highlights her impressive figure. I'm struck by how delightful her curves are from this angle. Each hip bops up and down as if bouncing to a silent drum. They produce their own music, dancing without needing a reason. While I'm distracted with her rear end I almost miss how swiftly she prepares the drinks. Something tells me she's done this before. Sandra sneaks a sultry glance over her shoulder, lips pouting the extra mile, and then turns to face me with a drink in each hand and shrugs. It makes her boobs seem like they're pouting at me as well.

'Stacey and I snuck up here once to pinch a couple of drinks. I think we were fourteen, fifteen maybe? Anyway it looks as though they still have the same cleaner.' She nods toward the fridge. 'The first vodka bottle I opened had been refilled with water.'

We laugh. I gratefully accept the drink. The coolness against my palm pacifies my nerves. I lift the glass to my lips and savour the heady smell of fruit. I exhale.

'So much better than beer,' I declare.

'Cheers to that,' she holds up her glass, which I greet with mine with a satisfying clink. Sandra saunters to the bed and kicks off her heels. She pats next to her and I gleefully respond, kicking off my shoes to slide onto the bed. The mattress greets me like a warm cloud of hugs. I take a moment to relax into the luxurious comfort, then sit up to look at Sandra. 'So, tell me more about yourself,' she prompts.

I shrug. 'There isn't much to know. I don't like sport, I don't like beer. I do like this though,' I say, holding up the glass.

'Do you have a girlfriend?' she dives in, straight for the jugular.

'No.'

'Boyfriend?'

'Nope.' *I wish*, I add to myself. I try to look at her out of the corner of my eyes to read from her face, but I can't without letting on that the question struck a nerve.

'Why not?'

'Well, school doesn't offer much prospect for a girl-friend, and the rest of my time I spend between work and homework, so I don't really get out much. I haven't had the chance to find anything that takes my fancy. What about you? Do you have that special someone tucked away?'

'No. Not anymore, anyway. I was with a guy for a few months but he turned to be a typical school kid. He got bored quickly and started searching for something else without realising he had started something with me. He wasn't a dick or anything; he just wasn't very grown up. So do you mean you've never had a girlfriend at all?'

I panic again. Admitting I'm a virgin is as much a threat to my mask of masculinity as being gay. I start to stammer out some made-up girlfriend credentials when she interrupts me. 'Hey, I told you, no pretending. Don't worry about it, it's all good.' She ponders for a moment, then evil blossoms across her face. 'Do you want to watch a dirty movie?'

'What!?' I choke on an ice cube. The cold pain hovers in my throat while I regain my composure.

'A porno?' she asks again.

'Girls watch pornos!?'

'Yeah, of course. We aren't all sweet and innocent until we get married. Some of us do things with our lives other than wait to have babies. Besides I think that's the only genre of film in this room.'

While I'm still recovering from my apoplexy, Sandra's hand slides down the edge of the quilt and pulls out a drawer under the bed. After a quick look, she starts reading off titles, '*Snow White and the Seven Horny Dwarves, Lord of the Strings, Georgia's Bush, Riding Miss Daisy, The Little Spermaid, Big Titties in Little China, Poke-her-hontas.*'

She looks up in disgust. 'They really need to come up with some better names. It's as if they aren't even trying anymore.'

'Um, the big titties one sounds like a safe bet. I don't think I could watch *The Little Spermaid*, it sounds way too much like a kid's flick.' She snickers at the word 'flick'.

'*Big Titties in Little China* it is.'

Sandra slides the disc into the television, dashes to the door, locks it and returns to my side on the bed. The heat of her body radiates against the side of my arm as she presses up close, much closer than we were before.

The movie swings into action almost immediately, and graphically so. It was skin and boobies jiggling in every direction. Slapping sounds, pounding flesh and primal groans speak in a wordless but clearly understood language. The hung male star howls his conquest at the moon as though they could hear him there—there's no sound barrier for pleasure. The women sing their siren song calling for 'more' and 'harder', but their praise of his prowess rings false. The action does little to tweak any arousal within me, and instead I'm transfixed by a sense of morbid curiosity. I'm vaguely aware, however, that the video does much more for Sandra. I try to interpret the signals she's sending, but I just don't have the right internal programming to unscramble the message, so I have no idea what she's doing.

I feel cornered. Sandra is definitely attractive, and I guess she thinks the same of me. She's stolen me away into this stranger's bed, and plied me with booze and porn. But she's practically a stranger herself, and this isn't how sex is supposed to happen—you're supposed to form some kind of connection. But Sandra just lies there, quivering gently and looking at me with expectation. But I don't know how to give her what I think she wants, I don't even know if *I* want to.

Suddenly, I'm scared as hell. I gulp down the remains of my drink. The glass was still mostly full, the drink sticks in my throat. I resist the urge to gag because I think I'll lose my dinner. I choke and cough to swallow it down, which Sandra notices and looks across to me.

'You alright?' she asks.

I can't respond so I simply look up at her. Our eyes meet, possibly in the corniest of ways, yet I feel some compulsion that tells me the most natural movement is forward. No questions linger through my brain anymore, and all I'm aware of is my body, and the body touching mine. Sandra knows what she wants and moves in to take it. Her lips collide with mine, latching onto each other refusing to move or allow any disconnection. We relax a little from the initial impact, though my heart is still in a flurry, belting itself inside out. Sandra's lips are soft and tender as she begins pecking away at my bottom lip. Her movements are precise and knowing, and I allow her to lead this dance. It's not her first time at the ball. A jabbing moistness demands to be let into my mouth. I surrender without a fight, and her tongue launches into the newfound land, marking its territory inside my mouth. Sandra wastes no time in pushing me back, then launches her whole body on top of mine. Her landing is awkward, crushing my erection as she tries to slide a leg either side of me.

My erection confuses me. I never expected it to come so quickly, not for a girl. But I have no control over the matter—my body knows what's happening and takes the required action. Sandra moans intensely when she finds proof of my arousal. I groan back, sheepishly—I feel the fool as I don't feel anything to groan about, but the mere hint of my pleasure sends Sandra into a mini frenzy. She whips off her outer layers of clothing and begins an assault on mine.

Very quickly only our underwear remains, and I realise the challenge before me. All boys must conquer the bra as a rite of passage to manhood. It may be overdramatic, but that's how it sounds when the guys talk about it. Sandra surrenders my lips, allowing my approach to the clip on her back. She clears my path with a quick flick of hair, and I trace my finger over her silky skin to discover the enemy latched firmly in its stronghold. I am David to this giant and this time it will be defeated. I follow instincts and squeeze the clip between my thumb and forefinger. It tremors and buckles, and then the straps fly free. *That was easy*, I think to myself. I don't know what all the fuss is about at school. Sandra's bra slides off her shoulders, exposing round breasts and cherry-red nipples. She pulls me in, pressing a breast toward my mouth. I follow, teasing the nipple, first with my lip and the jabbing it with the point of my tongue. Sandra responds, her body shuddering to its core. As I try to continue with foreplay, she pulls at my jocks, and when her goal is achieved she grabs steadily onto my cock. It pulsates in her soft hands as they gently caress back and forth like a soothing massage. It's not mind-blowing ecstasy but it is nice.

I lose track of time. Sandra breaks away from our rhythm to fish through the bedside drawers. My mind boggles as to what she's doing. Is this part of what girls need to do during sex? I have heard jokes about girls refusing sex because they have too much on their mind, but I'm sure that organising someone else's drawers is just too strange. My question is answered when she returns with a condom. I do know what that's all about. Even though sex ed in a Catholic school is heavy on the abstinence, they are smart enough to teach us about contraception.

Sandra's hands latch onto my shoulders and hoist me on top of her. Her legs ease apart to direct me in the required position.

'Here, put this on,' she says in the most seductive tone she could muster, handing me the condom.

I'm trembling as I tear at the packet. I try to maintain the mood and keep my movements smooth and deliberate. The condom slides on easily after a couple of misfires, then Sandra wraps me in her limbs and drags me down on top of her. Our breaths and chests are shared. Heat fires from the friction in our skin. Her hips gyrate, ready to take charge of my cock.

'Put it in,' her voice groans.

I follow her instruction. I reach down between my legs and find *it*. My hand grazes on moisture. A wave of excitement floods through me, electricity jolting my spine. Easing forward, I'm engulfed by her, swallowed in one movement. The thrill squeaks in her lungs, and mine.

Just like that I'm having sex. A few hours ago it seemed a distant impossibility, and here I am inside a girl, rocking my backside in a mixture of random motions, trying to achieve some vaguely understood goal. I think I enjoy this. I'm erect, and I'm inside a girl, and I feel a satisfying sense of achievement. Okay, it's not the mind-blowingly crazy-good reaction I'd been lead to expect from movies and change room bragging, but it's kinda pleasant. Nice even. It's not repulsive.

Sandra claws into my back and starts groping and gasping. Heat and moisture stroke along my cock. Sweat builds an extra glistening layer of moisture making each consecutive movement slide easier than the last. All of our hairs droop and tangle in a concoction of juices. A mixture of ripples and muscles greet my every forward thrust. She is choking on the air, her breaths hard and ragged. Her back arcs so her erect nipples press against my chest. I know this moment. We must be reaching the climax. Sandra tenses and shrieks, it generally sounds like it's a good thing, so I assume I'm doing something right. My body starts to react too, it's a sensation I know well. This time it's upon me without warning. The shivers and spasms suddenly take hold of my body as I shoot out a few short breaths and ejaculate.

My arms shake as suddenly my strength evaporates. I'm unsure what to do next. Do I lie on top of her or pull away and collapse next to her, I don't know the etiquette. I take the second option, easing out of her and then rolling to the other side of the bed away from the wet patch on the bed covers. A short giggle escapes her lungs.

'Good to finally meet someone who pays attention to what's going on,' she laughs. 'Coming from an all-boys school I had my doubts, but wow.' She slowly regains her breath. 'I suppose I should see where Stacey has ended up.'

She giggles again, louder, before offering a quick peck on the cheek, sliding off the bed, redressing and dashing out of the room. I'm in too much of a daze to pay attention, and as the doors slam behind her, I drop my head onto the bed. *I had sex*, I sigh to myself. A moan echoes nearby. I ignore it in the first instance thinking my brain is reliving my first time. But when it happens again I realise the porn film is still playing in the background. I look down at myself. I'm naked, a used condom hanging from my now sagging cock, and watching a porn film, apparently by myself. I freak, feeling like I've been abandoned in this awkward situation—*How the fuck did I get here?* My heart takes off for the millionth time this evening. I sprint to the television and hunt out the power button. I panic when I can't find it immediately, but with further searching I find it hidden underneath the console and clear the room of the sounds of sex. The silence calms me down a little. I pinch the base of the condom and try to yank it from my body, but it's gripped onto my skin and refuses to come away without a fight. I yelp in pain that ricochets through my body, then quickly bite my tongue—the last thing I want is to be caught in this position. I close my eyes and grit my teeth and slowly work it out (well, off) and once it's done I can relax a little and breathe another sigh of relief. Eventually I open my eyes again, to be confronted with the floor, and a fresh white patch blessing the otherwise maroon carpet with the contents of the now inside out condom.

'Shit,' I whisper. 'Shit, shit, shit, shit, fuck.'

I react without thought, pressing my foot into the puddle to rub it into the carpet. It disappears a little, but now my still warm spunk is oozing between my toes, and my panic begins to rise again. Confusion about my sexuality rages in a battle for attention with my shame for offending God with sex outside the bonds of marriage, and both are drowned out by the fact that I AM STARK NAKED IN A STRANGER'S BEDROOM HOPPING ABOUT WITH MY FOOT SMEARED IN MY OWN CUM HAUNTED BY THE MEMORY OF A RAIDED BOOZE FRIDGE AND THE WHIRRING OF A PORN DISC IN THE DVD PLAYER.

My mind finds first gear again and I set into motion. I hop delicately into the en suite and throw the condom into the toilet. I almost throw my foot in after it to rinse off the spunk. I decide against it and opt for toilet paper. It all flushes away and takes a little bit of my desperation with it. I only have to find my clothes and I'm home safe.

Well mostly anyway. I can still smell Sandra's perfume lingering on my skin and taste the remnants of her gloss on my lips. I snatch up my clothes and throw them on in some approximate order, then creep out of the bedroom praying that no one has noted my absence from the party.

V.

TIME FOR TRUTH, FOR SOME

'SANDRA Coleman?' Mark asks for the twentieth time today.

'Yes, Sandra,' I groan. Mark's stubborn disbelief about my rendezvous last week is starting to get insulting. 'And you were in a fight,' I remind him while glancing aimlessly across the tennis courts. Another group of boys are sitting at the far end arguing over a set of cards, or something like that. I can't be completely sure from this distance. Other than them, we have the tennis court benches to ourselves.

'Hardly, I was just breaking up an argument. I had nothing to do with it.'

'I heard you were the one to throw the final punch.'

'He wouldn't stop, what was I supposed to do? I didn't lay into him or anything like that. It was just enough to stop him.'

'And one of your teammates decided he liked the look of his car perched against a tree,' I add.

'Yep, it was a good party.'

Yep, it had been a perfect trifecta party, and the gossip channels are going crazy. I realise that this is what I had hoped for, so I could ride the associated glory for a while, just by having been there. I hadn't anticipated actually becoming the subject of the gossip. Still, I guess it could have been worse—there's no way I could hold my own in a fight like Mark, and Tristan had spent every cent he'd earned pimping the car he'd scraped against a gum tree. Somehow, almost immediately, word had raced around the school that I'd slept with someone. You could ask anyone about it, and they wouldn't skimp on the details. The details might not necessarily have been accurate, but no one let that curb their enthusiasm, which did lead to some interesting variations. I thought I'd managed to get back to the kitchen unnoticed, and then home without a hitch. But someone had found out, and now it was all over the school.

'But Sandra Coleman,' Mark repeats through a mouthful of his sandwich.

'Yep.'

'How did you even meet?' It has been an endless string of questions from Mark. This topic of me having sex has somehow distracted everyone, including Chris who hasn't even hinted at bullying in a while, probably because I'd now slept with more women than he had.

'I told you, she found me.'

'But then what? How did you end up, y'know, *doing it*?'

'We went up to the parents' bedroom to sneak a drink. She decided we were going to watch a porno and then we just went for it.' Mark grins, just as he has every other time we've talked about it. It's a little weird that he gets enjoyment from my sex story, but I don't think it's a sexual thing, I think it's just happiness for me.

'How did you go for it? You can't just go from watching a movie straight to sex. You must have some pretty special moves?'

'Not really. I didn't have to do that much. She made the move on me.' Mark coughs out a dry laugh.

'You lived the dream, mate,' he pats me on the shoulder. I'm a champion in his eyes. Well, he's my mate, so I guess he thinks that anyway, but this is something different. Now I'm a champion in everyone's eyes. I'd done the impossible and got a girl to come after me offering porn and a good time. Apparently that's some male fantasy, and now it's done I could have my face imprinted on the back of coins along with the heroes and monarchs of our nation. Apparently I'm worthy of that just for having sex. 'Yeah, I'm sure I have,' I mumble.

'What?'

'Nothing.'

'Sure thing,' he digs back into his sandwich and waits for me to continue. He knows me well enough to wait for something to be said.

'I guess.' I'm not sure where to start. My words become a fluster in my head, each beating the sides demanding my attention. 'I guess it wasn't that fantastic.'

'What!?' Mark spits out half his sandwich in shock. The sudden noise rouses the attention of the guys at the far end of the court from their squabble over cards, who look up and laugh at the spectacular showering of food.

'What yourself,' I cringe, hoisting my feet out of the line of fire.

'It wasn't that fantastic?' he wipes his chin free of

ham. 'You had sex with a girl. How can that not be fantastic?'

'I don't know. It was nice and all. I guess I just wasn't that into it.'

Mark stares at me in disbelief. I agonise over my next words. My instincts tell me to retreat, to turn around and sprint in the other direction away from the harm of the truth. Mark's eyes are questioning, yet still command the kindness I have come to know over the years. I've never known him to break a confidence, or speak maliciously. And the only time he's ever judged me after telling him something was when he was when I'd kept the news of dad being in the hospital to myself for so long. I just didn't want anyone else to worry about me, but I could tell that he'd been hurt that I hadn't shared my fears with him. He's giving me that same look now. His eyes search mine for an answer, for that little hidden truth he now knows is in there somewhere. I'm so used to Mark the jock that it really takes me off guard when he expresses compassion and understanding.

I open my mouth but instinctively choke on my words. *I almost outed myself.* My stomach churns, ready to empty itself. A priest might be able to understand me, that's their job, but how could a sportsman, some poster boy for masculinity? If I told him, how could he see me as anything but weak, something different and untrustworthy? Tears force their way into my line of sight, and the image of Mark's penetrating gaze blurs. And it's that look that convinces me I can't keep this secret to myself any longer, and I don't want to. I push back my fear and its petty demands, and blurt out my truth.

'I don't think I'm into it in general,' I stutter. My nerves ride higher; the altitude sucks oxygen from my lungs. I try to stifle any sign of nervousness to await Mark's response before giving anything more away. Mark offers nothing but a blank stare.

'Huh?' he struggles out.

I stare back at him, trying to coax at least a little more than a 'huh' out of him, hoping he'll say it so that I don't have to. How can he not understand? Do I have to spell the problem out for him?

'I'm not into sex, so much, in that way. Like with Sandra.'

Nothing ticks over in his eyes. The caring stare glazes over. I sigh, surrendering to frustration.

'With girls,' I blurt out in a whisper, 'I think I'm gay'.
'You're what!?'
'Gay.'
'As in gay? *Gay* gay?'
'Yes, *gay* gay.' How many gays can there possibly be?
'Oh.' Mark's attention on our conversation fades. He returns to the remnants of his sandwich and forces it into his mouth. I wait, the anti-climax looming up behind me. Each crunch of lettuce grinds on my ears. I need to know more about what he's thinking. I need to know if he will react badly to this news. If my best friend can't understand me, then who could? But Mark doesn't seem inclined to hurry and put me out of my misery. He just

keeps on chewing, and my mind is left to wander. I'm not entirely sure myself that I'm gay. I mean, I did have sex with a girl, so maybe I have a chance at bisexuality instead. Surely that's better in God's eyes than being full-blown gay. And maybe it would make having a family possible for me. I ponder and continue to stare as Mark finishes his sandwich, urging him to speak with my eyes.

'What?' Mark finally responds.

'I um … just told you I'm gay,' I prompt.

'So?'

'Is that it? So?'

'Is there anything else I'm supposed to say?'

'I don't know. I thought you would react in some way. A beating, perhaps. Or rejection—that's a common one. But "so". That wasn't a response I expected in this event.'

'This event?'

'Yes, this event. Me coming out to someone.'

'Am I your first?'

'Not really. I told Father D in confession.'

'Oh, okay.' Mark turns from me and rifles through his bag in the hunt for more food. Nothing else registers on his radar while there's food on offer, it's as though some inner primate takes over. It sniffs out a banana from the hidden depths of the bag and tentatively extends its arm forward, knowing any sudden move could frighten away the prey. Then with the banana in hand, it retreats to the safety of a tree to peel the fruit and indulge in this seasonal delight. The first bite is always slow, to be certain the banana is in fact a banana and not tainted in anyway. Then the rest is consumed with gusto and Mark, the human one, returns.

'Well?' I grow impatient.

'Well what?' he forces out through the mouthful of banana.

'Aren't you going to say anything else about what I just said?' I can't even bring myself to use the word *gay* again. It took too much out of me the first time, and it's easier to fall back on the familiar mode of repression.

'Um, so… what?' he shrugs.

'And?'

'And what else is there to say but "so"? It doesn't change anything. I'm glad you told me, but that's about it. You're gay, so what?'

I'm stunned. This is definitely not the scenario I projected in my mind a thousand times. Yelling and bawling and screaming and denial and hatred and fear of being hit on: that had all been planned for, but none of this.

'Is that it? You don't have any questions about it?'

'Well I could if you want?'

'Well, I don't know. I would have assumed everyone had questions when told something like that.'

He shrugs and indulges me. 'Okay then. Um, how do you know you're gay?' he throws the question into the air without real effort. It's enough bait for me.

'Well, I don't know for sure. It's guys I'm attracted to, but the first time I had sex was with a girl.'

'So you're not gay? You haven't even been with a guy?'

'I think I'm gay, or at least bi, but I can't be sure. I

haven't been with a guy yet. It was fun with Sandra, but nothing that fantastic.'

'Do you want to be with a guy?'

'Yes.'

'Do you fancy me?' This is more along the lines of the questions I had been planning for.

'No.' As I say it I surprise myself to realise that it's true. I was painfully aware that Mark was very attractive, but he was my mate, and that's all I wanted him to be. 'Nope, you don't have to worry about that.'

'I'm not worried. I was curious to hear the answer.'

'I bet you were, jock boy. You know you're hot.'

'Come off it, I'm not. I don't have girls throwing themselves at me.'

'You do, you're just too blind to see it.'

Mark stares at me doubtfully for a moment, and then, 'Do you have a type?'

'Hah, look at you; you know more about it than I do. I don't really know yet if I have a type. Possibly.'

'Oh, okay.' Mark continues to watch me, waiting for me to continue. The words inside my head are backlogged to the point of bursting out, peering over the edge but not daring to take the plunge to be vocalised. Mark notices, and fishes with further questions, possibly hoping to find the right one to burst the dam and spill all the words. 'Have you told your parents?'

'Not yet.'

'Are you going to?'

'Probably. I want to tell them, but I'm worried they'll

reject me.'

'Why would they do that?'

'I don't know. Why wouldn't they?'

'They can't reject you for something like that.'

'Are you sure?'

'Yeah, they're your parents. As if they'd give up on their child. They might not be completely happy about the situation, but I doubt they would actually disown you for something like that.'

'I guess you're right. Being anti-gay is one thing, but being anti-your-own-son would be pretty heartless.'

'What about school?' Mark asks.

'What do you mean?'

'Are you going to be out at school? Are you even allowed to be openly gay at a Catholic school?'

'I would think so. Father Donovan doesn't seem to have an issue with it. He was very understanding.'

'Are you going to be Catholic still?'

I open my mouth to respond instantly, but only a timid puff of air emerges. I still don't know how to respond to that question. I want the answer to be yes, but with everything the Bible seems to say I don't feel like it's up to me.

'I'm not sure,' I force myself to speak again, vocalising my thought process. 'I feel like I have to choose between the two. I can't see the church allowing me to be both. Either way I'll keep the church teachings close to my heart, but I think I'll have to remove myself from the church in the end. And maybe that's the best thing I can do to be faithful to the church. I can't choose the way I feel about guys, I think, but I can choose to leave the church and keep it pure.'

'Dude, don't be so harsh on yourself. You're one of the best people I know, and the church should be doing what it can to keep you. You could always speak to someone, y'know.'

'What? Like who?'

'I'd start with Father Donovan, you said he was understanding. He might be able to help you out, if you'd only ask,' Mark offers.

'Perhaps, but how would I even bring it up with him?'

'You've already done it once. Just go ask to speak to him in his office. Heaps of guys go to him when they have trouble with their assignments and stuff.'

'What assignments?'

'Religion assignments.'

'People ask for help with those? They aren't even marked. He just writes a comment.'

'Some of us like to take on the extra learning when we can.'

'Wait, it's you? You speak to Father D about religion assignments?'

'Yeah, of course.'

'Of course?'

'Yeah, a lot of athletes praise God in thanks for their skills, and a lot of sporting clubs hold to Christianity to increase team bonding and seek out areas for improvement. I think faith will be as important as athletic skill when it comes to being a professional sportsman, playing for a league club and being a part of the team.'

'Huh, I've never really thought about it like that. I could never see the point of sprinters trying to be the fastest in the world decked out in a bunch of gold crosses. Imagine how fast they could run without the extra weight.'

'Probably slower,' Mark responds thoughtfully. 'The weight of the jewellery doesn't matter so much as what it means to them. They wouldn't be able to run as fast without their faith that God believes in them and their talents just as they do in him.' Mark's dedication to his sport and his faith, and the way he tied them together blew me away a little bit. All I could do was sit and stare, so he continued on. 'The crucifix is a symbol of God's presence, and without it His spirit in their life and in their sport fades. Every athlete needs a way to get into the right headspace, and faith is a great way of doing that.'

'So it's not just touching each other on the butt?'

'Don't be a dick. When you're playing with a team, my teammates will slap me a few times before we run out of the change rooms, and I'll slap them too. It gets us psyched up, and reminds us we're part of a team of guys we know will have our backs. Don't hate on it just because you don't understand it.'

'Seriously?' I blurt out in a mixture of shock and laughter. 'You get slapped on the arse by a heap of guys?'

'Of course. I used to get fired up toward the end of the game if scores were close, or when I was tackled or something, and then I would wipe the floor with the other team. But when we slap each other before we get onto the field, it gets my blood pumping and I can go out with guns blazing.'

'So, it's a bunch of guys who like having other guys slap them,' I observe.

'Was that your attempt at a straight joke?'

'Kinda, do you think it works for me?'

'No way. You should stick to what you're good at—making coffee,' he slaps me on the shoulder with a loud thud.

'Come on,' I complain. 'I'm not your teammate. You don't get to whack me.'

'Dude, you're my best mate. You're my teammate all the time, not just on a sports field. You need to know that I'll always have your back. And sometimes, I'm sure I'll need to get you fired up.'

I'm blown away again. I'd come into this conversation thinking that Mark was going to change the way he treated me, as though he would see me as less of a man somehow. I assumed gay guys would be treated as girls, untouchable except in very specific circumstances. But Mark had just shown me that I'm still one of the guys. The relief was dizzying.

The siren bellows in the distance, calling us back to the mundane routine of school life. We collect our packs and head for English class in silence. Our feet fight against the routine, dragging heavily on the grass outside the tennis courts, their rebellion futile before the certain doom of literature studies.

Distracted by my fate, I'm taken by surprise by a sudden collision to my chest that hammers the breath from my lungs. I gasp in shock. My ribs contract as though they were bending like a branch to the point of snapping, or at least it feels that way.

'What the fuck was that for?' I hear Mark's voice cut through my pain and bewilderment. I blink clear the tears and confusion to discover Chris and Mark shoving each other back and forth.

'He's a fucking faggot,' Chris spews out, his mouth an ugly snarl.

'Are you on crack?' Mark fires back.

'You're on his fucking crack. You're a poofter as well,' he thuds the heels of his hands into Mark's chest. I hear a pop but Mark's doesn't even blink. He's trained for this. He strikes swiftly, pushes Chris off balance and slams his fist into Chris' cheek. I can see Mark pulled his punch, trying to shock Chris into backing off rather than hurt him. Chris isn't clever enough to see it, though. 'That's how a fag would punch,' Chris rallies his bluster to maintain his bravado-fuelled alpha warrior mask, but he sounds pathetic even to me. His hand cradles his cheek, and his cover is blown. I can see tears well up in the corners of his eyes, a catastrophe to happen in front of the ever-present onlookers eager for a show.

'You need to get over yourself, Clapham,' Mark orders Chris. 'Not everyone is going to stand for your shit.'

Chris waves a feeble finger at Mark, trying to cover his defeat. He knows he's lost. The final glare is straight at me, threatening revenge. The initial twinge of vulnerability is beaten back by the fact that I have Mark at my shoulder.

'Rack off already. Aren't you late for class?' Mark looms with intimidation.

With his tail drawn tightly, Chris scurries away. I straighten up as the wind hesitantly returns to my chest.

'Thanks,' I mutter warily.

'Don't mention it,' Mark slaps my back, knocking the wind out of me again, but this time it feels good, reassuring. 'I'm sure you'd do the same for me.'

'I can't do what you just did.'

'We're mates. We don't let the other cop shit in front of us. You were caught off guard and I helped out. No big deal.'

'You've just got a taste for blood from the weekend and are pumped for another fight,' I try to lighten the mood. It works.

'Hell yeah!' Mark jokes. 'Can't get me enough of punchin',' he grunts sarcastically.

'Whoops, someone's using up all the testosterone, share some with the rest of us.'

'Ha, you wish.' His face contorts quickly from smiles to serious. 'You know hitting someone isn't my favorite thing to do.'

'I know, but I appreciate it. I guess it was necessary to help me out.'

'It was, and I would never attack when it's not needed. It's the same with a footy match. You knock them down when they have the ball and help them out once the ball's gone. You never lay into someone for no reason.'

The blank stare returns. I never realised how much thought Mark puts into other people. He can be quite rough and tumble out on the field, but he always stops to offer a hand to the opponent and help them up. But I didn't know he made such a point of it, to almost worship the idea of good sportsmanship in his daily life.

'That's a good motto to live by,' I encourage.

'You think so?'

'Yeah definitely, nothing is gained by leaving people all over town with grudges.'

'True. See you do look out for me as well. I'm a bit stronger, you're a bit smarter.' I feign a warm chuckle. 'I guess Chris won't be speaking to you for a while. Is that the first time he's hit you?'

'Second. This week anyway.'

'Does he know about you? You know—what you just told me?'

'No, I don't think so. I think he's just paranoid and takes it out on me. I guess I'm an easier target than someone selected in every sports team known to mankind.'

'That sucks. But I don't think he'll want to get to you for a while.'

I hope that Mark is right. He sounds confident, but the hatred overflowing from Chris' eyes told another story. I knew my encounters with him would not be over; his fist, my face, a tragic love story.

VI.

CUPID'S DEMON UNLEASHED

I LOVE the smell of coffee in the morning. After a horrendous slog through miserable streets to catch a predawn bus, the smell of coffee is an angel's fart. It's heady and intoxicating with a bite. Here at the tail end of winter, the darkness has become like a friend. Well maybe more of an acquaintance, like that quiet kid in maths class that I don't talk to but nod at when we pass in the hall. I peer into the familiar darkness, glaring wearily at headlights until one manifests into the bus. And then the darkness glares back through the bus window as the sleeping streets pass by. I'm still groveling and moaning by the time I walk into work, welcomed by the blessed aroma of coffee and confronted by an overwhelming morning rush to manage with little help from Jenna.

As manager, Jenna feels her work in the office takes priority over actually serving customers. Her approach is baffling. Instead of helping us sell coffee, which keeps us in business—and more importantly pays my wages—she takes herself off the floor to spend hours in front of a computer doing only a few minutes' work and doesn't replace herself with someone else in the shop. So I spin through the shop with the grace and fury of a hurricane. Milk splashes across counter tops, paper cups patter rhythmically on to the floor, and still I maintain a passive and caring voice to ask our dear *guests* their orders.

Luckily Daniel is due in twenty minutes. I'll be grateful when he arrives, even though we're not the best of friends. Surprisingly, even for him, he's managed to hold onto the fact that I cut his lunch serving the hot jocks, making it the longest time he's focused on one thing at work.

Despite buzzing on overdrive through the increasingly hazardous mess, I'm pleased to be able to ignore the new niggling sensation that runs its finger down the edge of my spine. Pleasure and longing string my nerves tight to the point that strumming them would snap fingers. Yearning balls a fist in my throat, teasing me with fantasies and stuffing my chest full of thick air. I think this feeling is my first real crush, and it's on a guy. Not a vague longing for a celebrity or someone else far out of reach, but an intimately personal feeling for Mark, my best friend. He's someone who I spend most days with, who I can physically touch by simply reaching to my left in class. And a month ago I could have done just that without a second thought, but since then spending time with Mark has felt awkward. Ever since he defended me against Chris these new feelings started. Nothing he does can be flawed by anyone; he's become the perfect man. And so he's invaded my dreams and desires. It's gotten to be quite distracting.

'Sorry I'm late,' Daniel declares as he walks in five minutes early. 'The bus driver was a douche and kept stopping for people at every stop. We were already full enough but he kept packing them on. I had a dude's fat ass in my face for most of the trip and I swear he farted. Either that or he always smells that bad.'

His ranting is a welcome distraction from my own thoughts.

'Is she in her office again?' Daniel whines. I nod. 'She always does that. Have you been flat out?' I nod again, exasperated. 'She did that to me yesterday. Disappeared when the morning rush started. I tried calling her but she didn't come out to help so I did the work of three or four people by myself. Why am I expected to do everything, especially when there's someone else in the office that could easily help out?' He spontaneously grows bored. 'So, what's the goss?' he turns toward me.

I shrug. 'Nothing new, I guess.'

'Seriously, nothing ever happens in your life.' *Got laid, beaten up, and now I'm crushing on my best mate, what have you done lately?* I think to myself. 'No girlfriend, no boyfriend,' he jabs. 'Not even a drop of alcohol on your nights off. You would have to be the perfect Catholic schoolboy.'

'I doubt that.'

'Ha! You, not perfect? You don't do anything interesting. Jesus would love you for being boring. He was the same. All he did was hang around,' Daniel holds his hands out in his crucifixion pose. His tongue pokes out limply in emphasis. 'Nah, nah, I joke. I shouldn't mock religion, one of them is bound to be right in the end so might as well be neutral.'

'Yeah, 'cause that went well for the angels.'

'Huh?'

'The fallen angels?'

'Doesn't ring a bell.'

'The angels who refused to pick a side in the battle for heaven. God damned them to the gates of hell for not choosing His side.'

'That's a bit harsh. Isn't he supposed to be all forgiving and loving and stuff?'

'Yeah, I guess so. But when his creations refused to help he decided to make an example out of them. That's one interpretation anyway. I guess I could be wrong. I don't exactly listen in those classes anyway.' *Except to the parts that are relevant to my personal dilemmas.*

'It's all interpretations, and not just religion, but life in general. You just have to look at things from a different angle and it can work in your favour.'

The unexpected thoughtfulness from Daniel is a rare insight. From the blank glistening in his eyes and the concentration on steaming the milk, I doubt he realises he's said something that helps me. It's all down to interpretations. I just have to find the one that works for me. I still can't be sure that I'm gay, even though I'm now *out*, let alone work out if my religion and God are just testing me with this man-crush on Mark.

My pocket vibrates suddenly, sending shivers up my leg. I don't usually receive messages. I keep my phone close at work so I can scroll through my feeds when it's quiet. I wasn't expecting a text, particularly at this time of morning. I sneak to the corner of the shop, my back deceptively to the customers and the office door. Daniel knows this drill with mobile phones, he created it.

'I didn't realise you had friends,' he mocks.

I ignore him and slide out my phone. The guilt rises immediately as the device eases out of my pants. I focus on concealing my actions from passersby. The phone lights up at my touch, flashing repeatedly with a gaudy *look at me* into my eyes. I open the message and am surprised to find it's from Sandra. We haven't spoken since our fling and now she's contacting me directly.

'Hi, this might be weird but it's Sandra, from the party a while ago. I asked around for your number. I couldn't help but keep thinking about our night together and was thinking we might be able to catch up again sometime. Possibly for the movies. I'd liked to see where things could go,' the message reads.

Awkward. I wonder if I've been completely clueless not to see a girl was interested in me. I give Mark shit about that all the time about missing all the signs. I guess she was pretty quick to duck from the scene so I didn't have much to go on, but I had no idea she might be still thinking about me. I wouldn't have thought of her at all if I hadn't had to keep telling Mark the story, and definitely hadn't thought about contacting her. I've been too busy thinking about myself and my own sexuality. I did have sex with a girl and now I've told my best friend I'm gay. How would that make her feel if she ever found out? She was the first (and possibly last) girl I'd have sex with. The encounter with Sandra was pleasantly enjoyable, but my feelings for her are nothing like the feelings I've developed towards Mark. There's something stronger, more urgent, about my feelings for Mark that I can't quite describe. I actually want to spend more time with him, even if it's just to be in his presence. The date Sandra's asking for might be fun, but I doubt it will be the beginning of anything good.

'So what does your girlfriend want?' Daniel chimes in.

'Huh? What?' I splutter out.

'Ha! I'm just kidding, sweetie. You should have seen your face. It was like you'd been caught wanking by your mother. Priceless.'

'No, just stuff I'm not sure how to deal with,' I respond lamely.

'Ooh, how intriguing. You can tell you old friend Daniel, I'm fantastic with advice. But not so much with secrets so you'd better not tell me anything you want kept quiet. But then I do love gossip, and you still owe me.'

'Fine,' I sigh, thinking he might be able to help in some way. If not, at least it would give us something to talk about for the rest of the shift other than how much he spent on his latest pair of shoes. He's already bragged that it was well over two hundred dollars, but I don't want to have to hear it again. 'I met this girl at a party, and now she wants to hang out and "see where things will go". But I don't.'

'Ha, I knew it was about a girlfriend. You're so clueless it's adorable.'

'She's not my girlfriend. We've only met once a few weeks ago and that's it. We haven't spoken since. Well, until she texted me just now.'

'Oh, so a stalker girlfriend then? Or did you give her your number?'

'Nope. I don't know where she got it from. She said she asked around, and it must have been from someone I know because not many people have my number.'

'Creepy, but a good sign. Shows she's definitely interested.'

'How can that be good when I'm not interested?'

'Trust me, I've been around. It pays to have a few people interested, because then you'll seem more attractive to someone you *are* interested in.'

'That's just gross. I just want to let her down without hurting her.'

'You don't. You can't.'

'What?'

'Rejection always stings a little, you can't avoid it. And the longer you put it off the more it will hurt, so just do it now while there's no actual attachment.'

'You might actually be onto something. So, what do I write back?'

'Get out your phone and type this: "Hey, it was nice to meet you and I do find you a cool person. But I'm not in a good place to take things further." And then you send it and thank me because I'm awesome.'

I focus on the message for a moment, only a couple of sentences but more than enough to get the message through. I have nothing to lose. Neither did I feel like I had anything to gain, but my message wouldn't be a cricket bat hitting at Sandra's ego. *Only a slight deflation*, I reassure myself, and besides I have enough to think about as it is with this new crush that's been developing. I hit the send button and the message is away into the aether. There's a jolt as a seemingly instant reply vibrates in my phone. A message beams on the screen.

'That's cool, just thought I would ask,' it says.

'That was easy,' I mumble to Daniel.

'What'd she say?'

'She says she's cool with it. Sounds like she was going out on a limb or something like that. No harm in trying I guess.'

'Yeah that's true. I think you're forgetting one last thing.'

'What's that?' Daniel waves his head around to gloat about his success. An almost angelic hue swarms around him from the overhead lights. 'Oh, thank you,' I say, satisfying his requirements.

The workday soon blurs into the next day at school. 'Hey,' Mark greets me as I step through the gate.

My stomach lurches, churning into a squirming mess of worms. I don't dare look at his face, his beautiful, kind, chiseled face. Dealing with a crush isn't supposed to be like this, is it? Surely not to the point that I can't even look him directly in the eyes?

'Hey,' I throw back at him, saved by the knee-jerk response.

'Are you feeling okay? You look a bit squeamish.'

I want to come clean, to tell him about the development in my feelings. I resist the urge, for now anyway.

'I'm not sure. I might need to go have a chat to someone in the office for a quick second.'

'Who? Are you finally going to go and talk with Father D again? Good for you.'

'Yeah,' I say, jerking my head in the direction of the office. I feel bad letting him believe a half-truth, but it just seems easier to do so. As I duck off, my mind projects a sweet fantasy of Mark calling after me, heartbroken and revealing his desire to be with me forever. In reality, he grunts then turns and wanders off without a second thought.

The office door slides open automatically, flushing the entrance in a mist of incense. It's common knowledge that the receptionist is a firm believer in meditation and prayer as stress relief. It seems to me that bringing her way of life into the office is forcing her smelly beliefs onto others. I choke silently on the aromatherapied air, marching on through a virtual cloud of roses that strikes at my eyes while a fiery sensation leeches into my skin. My lungs threaten to burst for air, but I force them to remain trapped behind my ribs. Just as I feel I can't bear the stench any longer, my destination appears in my sights, and I quicken my steps to make the last leap to freedom.

'It can be quite overwhelming, can't it,' Father Donovan observes calmly from his desk as I stumble into the room, gasping for air. He doesn't look up while he finishes typing on his computer. 'I'll just finish my email and be right with you. Have a seat. There's plenty of fresh air in here. I keep the window open even during these nippy days.'

I take the offered seat, and the wooden frame instantly punishes my back. I arch my spine to accommodate my posture to the chair while waiting for Father Donovan. This is only the second time I've been in his office, the first to return a set of pens he lent me for the day. I'd forgotten all of mine after attempting an art assignment at home, and when I gave them back I came into this very dull room consisting of brown wood everywhere. The humming of the computer played the only tune this room would ever hear. The most prominent artwork in the room is two slices of wood stuck together to form a cross. This bare Catholic symbolism dictates the colour scheme for the entire room. Not even the books in their shelves offer any variation in colour. Somehow I always believed Father Donovan to be a quiet man with little need for stimulation, but I never thought he would be as uninteresting as this.

'How can I help you today?' Father Donovan begins with a final click of his mouse.

'I have a bit of a problem and thought I should come talk to someone.'

'Well, that's my job. I'm not exactly paid for it, but that's why I'm here.' I stare blankly. 'That was a joke. I am paid.' Still nothing registers in the humour department of my brain. 'Not even a little smile? Well, I guess this is a serious topic for you. Fire away then.'

'Well, um,' I pause for a moment. All the words I need mull around my brain like sheep, just waiting for the first to step out and onto my tongue so the rest can follow. 'It's about the topic of my confession earlier this year.'

'Your conflict with religion?'

'Yes, and me being gay.'

'Yes I remember. Are you still having trouble understanding some things?'

'Yeah, but that's not why I'm here. I have another issue that involves me and another boy. I need some… guidance. It's awkward and I don't know what to do. I've never felt this way before. It's becoming too much for me to understand. I don't know if I have any control anymore. I don't even know if you're the right person to talk to. I mean, you're a mouthpiece for God, for the Bible, for the church, how could you be the right person to talk to. You're at least someone though, and that's why I'm here, to talk to someone.'

'Slow down one second,' Father Donovan's confidence soothes my overexcitement. 'I'm not entirely sure what you're talking about. It all sounds very pressing, but you're going to have to spell it out for me.'

'Right, sorry. Okay. Here goes. Promise not to condemn me for any of this?'

'I promise.'

'I think I have a crush on my best friend and it's driving me mad.' I squeeze my eyes shut in a vain attempt to protect myself from what is about to happen. Surprisingly, at least to my current state of mind, nothing negative comes.

'A crush?' he answers calmly.

'I think so. I can't be sure. I've never felt this way before.'

'Okay, explain to me what you've been feeling.'

'I think about him all the time. My stomach feels like it's about to launch into space whenever I'm near him. Sometimes it becomes so much that I can't look at him without being engulfed with guilt.'

'That does sound a bit like a crush.'

'You think?'

'Have you thought that maybe it's not a crush, but that what you feel for him is admiration.'

'How do you mean?'

'Well, when did you start feeling this way?'

'When he stood up for me,' I said, and proceeded to tell Father Donovan about the altercation between Chris and I, and how it had ended.

'Chris is that thug in your grade?' My eyes sheepishly find the floor in the office. I had just thrown Chris to the wolves without even meaning to. But then Father Donovan had already identified him as a thug. Even so I still felt a bit guilty for outing him. 'Don't worry about Chris,' Father Donovan continues. 'He won't catch any trouble from me, unless I catch him myself. It's unfortunate that you'll come across bullies like Chris in almost any setting, and that's not your fault, you've done nothing to deserve it. Sometimes people just hate because they've never learned a better way to deal with their own issues. But sometimes you will also come across their opposite—someone who will stand up for what's right, no matter what. So maybe that's what's happening here. Your friend did something quite brave. He stood up for you, came to your rescue, and placed himself at risk of physical attack and ridicule in doing so. It was quite a heroic act, and maybe that's how you feel about him now—the way you might admire a hero. And now you are nervous being around him because of this new status. It's easy to be confused by these new feelings and feel uncertain about how to act around him. Does that sound about right?'

'Yeah, pretty much, I guess. But how do I tell the difference between a having a crush and simply admiring someone and looking up to them?'

'That's for you to work out. You're the only one who knows what you're thinking and feeling. Whatever it is I'm sure you will work out the best action for you. But if you need, I'm always here to talk to. As a priest my hours are flexible, so I'm available any time you might need to talk, not just at school. Well, except on Thursday nights. I have the night off every week to pursue my own interests.'

'Oh, okay. Thanks for the offer. I think I might be okay for now.'

'You're welcome. You might need to head off to class now. The siren is about to sound.'

I wander mindlessly from the office. I don't even notice the incense burning my tonsils as I leave. Could that be all it is? I admire Mark for standing up for me? I thought it would have to be a crush. It was the only way I could explain it to myself. Now that I've explained it out loud, it does make a lot more sense. The sensation of a heavy lump in my chest that was the potential crush on Mark morphs into mist and floats out of my system with every breath. I don't feel the burden of this crush anymore, and the admiration seems easier to carry, underneath the friendship I already have with Mark.

''Sup?' And suddenly there Mark is again, constant and assured.

'Nothing,' I answer, joining him as we enter geography. I'm glad to realise that I mean it.

'You bolted pretty quickly. I just thought things might be a bit weird for you at the moment?'

'What do you mean weird?'

'Dude, you just came out. Things are bound to be weird.'

'Oh, that. I think I'm fine with that. Mostly anyway. I just had to talk to Father D about something before I forgot. I thought you didn't have a problem with the gay thing anyway.'

'Of course I don't. I just thought you might like to talk to someone about it at some point. Must be tough with all the pressures and all that.' His voice turns to a whisper as the class quiets down. 'I don't have any idea what this process is like for you. But it's gotta be hard to do it alone. It might be good to share it with someone and get it out, and I thought that person could be me.'

'Nah, I should be good with all that. Thanks anyway. I just had something to get off my chest.'

'Anything I know about.'

'Just spoke about you.'

Mark snorts. 'Good on ya. Talking to a counsellor about me.' He smiles, displaying each of his perfect, sparkling teeth.

'Yeah, all about you,' I stir, the blend of crush and admiration duel inside of me for top position.

'Good way to make a bloke paranoid. You had mostly good things to say then?'

'Yeah, probably. You can't say anything wrong when you're talking to a priest anyway.'

'True, very true.'

Mark tunes out of our conversation ready for the lesson on erosion. His geography book is scarred by a collection of scribbles and misshapen stick figures. He doesn't seem to realise I wasn't joking about the topic of my conversation with Father Donovan. It doesn't matter either. I'm starting to believe what Father Donovan said was true. It isn't so much a crush. I notice I can still see his flaws when I think about it, the dent in the back of his hair where he can't see in the mirror, his tag out the wrong way, the ripe odour that tails him after phys ed. All minor details, but surely a crush would mean I would need to overlook details like that. I know my understanding of relationships is mostly informed by romantic films and books that idealise romance as a blissful state where everyone is blessed and happy and nobody farts. It was the perfect world of fantasy, which I guess is where you live when you have a crush. But I was still here in the real world, a world where I can now—almost completely—accept that I don't have crush on my friend. After all, now that I've thought about it I realise I don't have the strong desire to actually have sex with Mark. I'm guessing that's kind of essential for being with someone, again according to Hollywood.

VII.

HOW INCREDIBLY INAPPROPRIATE FOR A DINNER CONVERSTION

MEALS are never the most exciting event at the best of times. Unless you count the Christmas when Uncle Trevor drank half the wine and made out with the roast turkey before passing out in the coleslaw. That night almost turned me vegetarian, in fact I almost swore off food altogether. Luckily he didn't defile the ham, and there was plenty of that to go around.

At other times of the year I sit opposite Sarah and watch her move peas around hoping they will evaporate before dad forces her to eat them. Mum and dad share knowing glances and an unspoken joke down the other end of the table. I often wonder if it's some secret ingredient in their food they don't share with us that allows them to do that, but mum insists it just comes from being together for so long. I eat at the table and with maximum efficiency, and feel like I only eat out of necessity. I'm not here to enjoy the combination of pasta and leftovers from the fridge. I'm here to take on the energy needed to sustain myself for long enough to park my butt on the couch until the interesting television shows degenerate into reality programs that offer no real entertainment for me. That's the normal dinner routine at our house, and as far as I can tell it's the same at my friends' houses, with a little extra parental effort to engage me in conversation as their guest.

'How was your day, sweetie?' mum tries unsuccessfully to engage Sarah.

'Fine,' she responds neutrally.

'Just fine? There's nothing happening at school?'

'Just the usual.'

'The usual what?'

'Rumours and the like. Nothing worth talking about at the dinner table. It's all gossip.'

'Well, go on. It might be something interesting for us,' Mum tries to convey the image that she is now Sarah's best friend and they can dish dirt together. I almost cringe at the display.

'Well, there was something about this girl called Sandra.'

I flush red. Sarah is glaring at me. Smugness settles neatly on her lips when she sees the rumour confirmed in my face. Anger charges through my veins. It's a normal move for one of us to make over dinner, bring up a topic that will result in the attention shifting to the other sibling. But this one is personal, and excruciatingly embarrassing to talk about in front of parents. I want to scream at her, but I bite my tongue to the point of bleeding to hold in my displeasure.

'She's a year younger than me,' she continues, jutting her chin at me. 'She might be his age.' Hatred pours out of my eyes at her. She knows something and is about the break the silent truce between siblings to never use such powerful information against each other, especially without reason. Sarah must be bored. That would probably be enough reason for her. 'She got a bit drunk and wild at a party.'

'Oh, really. How delicious,' mum indulges Sarah's game, then turns on me, 'Do you know her?'

'I don't know anyone called Sandra,' I lie.

'You never know. You're of that age, pretty soon you should be bringing me a girlfriend home for my disapproval,' her smile lights the room but not the gloom I feel inside. This is going to be one uncomfortable dinner.

'I should be the one who gets to reject all my son's girlfriends,' dad snickers from his end of the table.

'No, no. That's the mother-in-law's job to be the evil one. You get to scare off Sarah's boyfriends. Go on Sarah, what happened to Sandra?'

'Nothing much,' Sarah continues. 'But it's been enough to keep everyone at school chatting for hours. She apparently hooked up with this guy at the party and then has been crushing on him ever since.'

'That's sweet, but it's not going to work out if you, what's the word, "hook up", when you first meet,' mum offers her unwarranted advice.

'Well it didn't apparently. She was completely heartbroken at school. Tears and all.' I can feel the guilt ready its saddle on my back. It knows it only has to jump on, and I won't attempt to buck it off. Sandra's despair is my fault; I deserve to be ridden into the dust.

'Oh my, that's unfortunate.'

'I know, right.'

'Do they know who the guy is? He must be quite a catch for her to get so upset about it,' mum muses. My only consolation is mum doesn't realise she's heaping fuel onto the fire.

'I hear he was quite nice to her at the time, but rejected her via text,' Sarah continues.

'Via what?'

'A text message, mum.'

'A what?'

'The messages the kids send through their mobile phones, Dear,' dad explains without looking up from his plate.

'Oh, a phone memo,' mum nods her understanding.

'Yes a phone memo mum,' Sarah rolls her eyes.

'But who would do that?' The leather slides with ease into the buckle of shame, the tightening strap crushing my chest. The stocky, thick legs of guilt straddle my sides, spurs pricking my hips.

'I know. It seems so heartless to reject someone like that. He could have at least made a phone call or something more real,' Sarah says.

'It's absolutely horrible. Who would do something like that?'

'She messaged first,' I spit out. The guilt rodeo is on, and I'm immediately defeated.

'What?' mum questions blankly. Dad shares her empty stare. Sarah beams victoriously. 'You do know Sandra.'

'Oh fuck,' I curse to myself.

'Of course he does mum. He's the guy she hooked up with.'

'You had premarital… relations, and rejected her with a memo?'

'A text message mum,' Sarah corrects. I just nod, gazing at the table.

'But why would you do that?' mum persists.

'Because I don't want to date her.'

'But a… a text message.'

'Ease up mum. It's not like I ended a year-long relationship with at text. Sandra texted me at work so I replied the same way just saying I didn't want to pursue anything with her.'

'Well, why not? I'm sure she's a lovely girl if you just give her a chance, what if she's pregnant now? What would her father say?'

'She's not pregnant, we used a condom.'

'Well, that was efficient of you,' mum interrupts, her tone a little heated, 'two sins for the price of one.'

'Steady on, mum,' I answer back. If we didn't use a condom then she could very well be pregnant, and wouldn't that situation be worse? Anyway, a minute ago you were eager to reject anyone I might bring home, and now you're taking her side? She probably is a nice person, but she's a stranger to me. And it's a bit creepy that she hunted out my number anyway. I don't know anyone who could have given it to…' I stop. The penny drops, pounding its weight onto the recognition centre of my brain. The smug expression on Sarah's face intensifies. Of course she was the one who gave Sandra my number, and now she's provoked this conversation in the last place I would want to have it. Mum focusses too greatly on her own questions to notice Sarah's self-satisfaction.

'What was wrong with her?' mum marches on.

'Nothing.'

'Then why didn't you go out with her?'

'Because I didn't want to.'

'That's not much of a reason.'

'Well that's it.'

'You haven't even gone on a date to find out if you do like her. Is there something else? Was it something she said at the party?'

'No, nothing she said.'

'Then, what is it?'

'Nothing.'

'Come on, you can tell us if she was mean or a little bit ugly.'

'No, mum.'

'No what?'

'No there's nothing more to add.'

'Yes there is. Come on. What was it?'

'Nothing.'

'Don't lie.'

'I swear.'

'Why won't you go out with her?'

'Because I'm gay.'

The words drown out every other possible sound. I instantly want to snatch them back out of the air, but it's too late, they've been heard. It isn't the first time I've said *it*, but I wasn't prepared for it to sneak out so cunningly. My ribs ache from the pounding of my heart, the bones in my chest creak to breaking point. It's done. I'm now out to my family. Rejection is inevitable—I can see it stealing over their faces. Sarah's jaw freezes into place. Her blank stare betrays the shock of the unexpected proclamation. Mum's lip quivers on the edge of further questions. Dad continues chewing on his pasta, staring intently at an article. I'm not even sure he heard me.

'Who has been saying that?' he asks (dammit, he did hear!) while sorting out which olive to next puncture with his fork.

'No one,' I croak.

'You don't need to listen to rumours about that sort of thing.'

'Uh, I don't think it is a rumour dad,' Sarah adds.

'Oh, okay,' dad finally looks up, flicks a glance around at the faces at the table, then returns to his food. 'You should probably say something to snap your mother out of her daze.'

'Mum,' I gather the most sympathetic look I can muster from beyond my watering eyes. Fear grips my stomach; I'm its plaything now. 'Is everything okay?'

'Yes, fine,' she responds as convincingly as a seventies movie robot. 'Just thinking about my next question. You've caught me off guard.'

'I know a question,' dad pipes up through the gallon of pasta sauce in his mouth. 'How do you know?'

'Huh?' I answer.

'That's something that has always interested me. How does someone know if they're gay?'

'Ah, I guess, how do you know that you're straight?'

'I just know.'

'Well it's the same answer for me. I just know.'

'Fair enough. How long have you known for?'

'I've been aware of it for a few years now, I guess.'

'Oh okay.' I wait for more from dad, but he's more tempted by another mouthful of pasta.

'I never thought you would be so... so fine with it,' I point out.

'Well, it's a little bit of a shock. I didn't pick it, that's for sure. But you're my son. Being gay doesn't change anything else I know about you,' dad says airily.

I well up with pride.

'I was convinced that you would reject me.'

'Reject you?!' mum blurts into the conversation. 'There's no way I could ever reject you. You're my child. Nothing will ever change that.'

Tears spout from her eyes, the moment too great to contain. Mum races around the table, knocking all obstacles out of the way to engulf me in an almighty embrace, as if she could protect me and hug away the demons of doubt and despair from my mind. For a few minutes, it works.

'Calm down dear,' dad offers, his voice void of real conviction. 'No need to frighten the boy,' he tries to joke.

'I know, I know,' mum regains some composure,

dusting herself off and returning to her seat. 'I just can't believe you would ever feel like we could reject you. There's nothing you could do that would make us do that.'

'He knows that now,' dad smirks. 'Charging at him like that may have been a little confronting for him though. Lads his age tend to avoid public hugs from their mums.'

'Don't be silly,' mum bashfully waves her hand at dad. 'We're in our own home and it's not every day your son mentions something like that to you. Good thing you didn't do it at Christmas, honey, there are enough bad events happening then as is. Not that this is a bad event, not that you being… this way is a bad thing. I just mean your uncle has done some stupid things at Christmas that have upset the family, so we generally have enough to deal with. Christmas should be for good memories not him screaming. Anyway, everything here's going to be fine, you just have to give us some time to adjust to this. You've no doubt known about this for a while and have had time to work your head around it.' Mum's return to composure and logical thought is faster than expected, dauntingly so.

'There isn't that much to work around,' dad interjects.

'Well there is a little bit. You see, we grew up in the time when being a—well, you know—a gay man meant being bashed or attacked for no real reason,' mum explains.

'I'm sure those times are over dear, for the most part anyway. I think being in town we should be fine. There are a lot of gay people here. He won't be picked on for being different.' Dad pauses for a moment, distracted by his own thoughts. 'I wonder if Uncle Herman is gay.'

'What?' mum asks.

'Well, he's always been single. Back in his day there was no such thing as homosexuality but there were a lot of bachelors who remained bachelors their whole life. I wonder how many of them are gay and don't know it because they've never considered it or don't believe it exists or even hide it from everyone.'

'I guess you won't be able to have kids,' Sarah speaks her mind to no one in particular. 'Not naturally anyway. I guess you could always adopt or something like that.' Her face contorts into the expression of a perplexed child, completely oblivious to the significance of coming out to your family. Instead her focus is the mothering side of her that for a couple years I doubted even existed. 'I've always imagined you with children,' she continues. 'I doubt something like this is going to stop you from being a dad.'

'I doubt it will too. I'm pretty sure I'll be a father one day, it's just a matter of when,' I say.

'And who with,' mum adds. 'Choosing the correct partner is very important for raising children.'

'Yes, and you did very well,' dad adds.

'I like to think I did, my children may beg to differ though,' mum responds. I force out a laugh. A single syllable chirps out, the falseness painfully obvious. Reality drifts away in the sea of disbelief and adrenaline. I've come out to my family. I can't imagine a bigger milestone in the development of my sexual identity. I'm gay and they still accept me, finding a way for religion to accept me can wait. *My family still loves me*, I scream in my head. The pride swells in my chest like a life jacket hoisting me above the waves. It rises and rises, lifting me completely out of the water. My mind remains anchored to the disbelief but my soul is freed to fly now that I don't have anything to hide or fear from my family.

I had expected the worst but nothing has changed. It was nothing more than a new piece of information, another pebble into the mountain that is me. Such a small detail, but I'd convinced myself if would be my undoing. I am myself and my family accepts me, all of me, as I am. Nothing can change their affection for me, although I may have forced Sarah to think twice before bringing up another interesting dinner conversation. They've completely forgotten about Sandra, she's little more than a distant memory, and I doubt Sarah with have the ammunition to fire out another piece of gossip like that for a while.

Later that night as I climb into bed I reflect on how my family's acceptance seems to have allowed a transformation within me. Not into a flaming drag queen or anything like that, but definitely into someone more energetic. I stare at the ceiling as I drift off to sleep, admiring the glow of the dark stars I stuck there when I was eight. I'm still energised when I wake early the next morning. I feel a sense of vitality, strength and courage lifting me up. I no longer have to spend endless energy hiding part of myself, and now that energy has to be spent in some fashion. It's only five o'clock in the morning but there's no way that I'll be going back to sleep anytime soon.

Boredom builds and begins the stumble into madness. I release myself from my bed sheets and ponder a wealth of possibilities. Maybe I could take up running to burn this energy that has found its way into my previously depleted stockpile. I've never ridden this wave before and don't know what to do. I could sprint around the house screaming Lady Gaga songs and waving a feather boa, or I could go for a walk around the block. I think the second option might please my parents, and the neighbours, a little more than the first. I wouldn't discount the Gaga option though. I have suspicions that Mr Keller down the street has a killer pair of heels and would gladly join me. He's never said anything to me of course, but my gaydar squeals like a pedestrian crossing every time I pass by him. (Get it? Gaydar, like radar but for gay people—the guys at school have even joked about their gaydars while showing how inaccurate they are).

I opt for the walk. The air is fresh to the point of a cold burn in my lungs. The morose grey-black of predawn does little to dampen the light glowing from my smile. It's the grin of freedom. Society and school had created a trap I felt I could never escape. That was until Sarah opened her trap and the dominoes of outing myself fell into place. I had prepared myself for every possible outcome of rebuttal and rejection other than the frankly underwhelming anticlimactic possibility of total acceptance. It was also a truly dumbfounding moment that had squeezed a dollop of numbing lotion on my tongue, leaving expression of mute shock and borderline idiocy. The idiocy had fortunately faded under the radiance of acceptance. I'm a lucky guy to have my family.

I'm not sure what to expect as I return home. The regular routine of semi-separation as we all followed our own interests after dinner meant I hadn't discussed much more with them. The house had become alive with activity in the hour I'd been gone. Granted the activity was mostly the buzzing of the coffee grinder and the hissing of the barista machine, as father sways droopy-eyed in the kitchen and mother fixates eagerly on a computer screen. Mum hears me come home and charges into the hall. Her hug this time is close to violent, her sobs penetrate horribly, and nothing slices you up easier than the tears of your mother.

'Everything okay mum? I just went for a walk.'

'I know, that's fine,' she chokes through her heaving sobs. 'I just read so many terrible things on the Internet. So many stories of parents rejecting their children because of their sexuality.'

'What are you doing on those sites?' dad stares half asleep over his mug of coffee, indulging in the fresh brew.

'I couldn't sleep so I thought I would read online how other parents deal with their children being gay and… and…' she bursts into another round of tears. Dad intervenes.

'That's not us, those people aren't us,' he comforts, a hand slowly rubbing down her back.

'I know,' she leans into his shoulder. A blown nose later and she has regained enough composure to talk. 'One mother guilted her daughter into trying to be straight and blamed her for all her illness and stress. The poor girl tried to commit suicide. Another lad was beaten by his dad and thrown out of home. Another rejected by her family and denied contact with her siblings. One forced into some boot camp to make him straight, spat on in public, targeted and beaten to the point of hospitalisation by school bullies. Another raped repeatedly by her father and brothers to force the gay out of her. Rape! Violence! Abuse! Rejection! And they call themselves parents!' mum borders on hysterical anger.

'It's not all like that mum,' I say. 'They're just the horror stories. It doesn't happen that much and besides that's not you. I know none of that will happen to me because you guys are my parents.'

'I know, I know. I just can't believe some people. These are their children they're hurting and rejecting. I can't believe anyone could do that.'

I really can't believe it either but I have to be honest, I feared it from my parents. No matter how much I know they love me and could never really do something like that, there was still the niggling pest nibbling away at my better judgment. No one in my family has come out before, I had no idea how my parents would react. It appears the claws are the first thing out. My mother is here to protect me and if she has any say she would be protecting all those other kids whose parents abused them. Time changes everything, or so I've discovered this far in my life. My parents will settle soon, my mum will stop looking up worst case scenarios online and we'll be able to talk about my sexuality openly no matter who is around. Well, that's my dream anyway and it appears to be on track. There's still one major issue to resolve about my sexuality, and it surprises me to realise it's not whether God accepts me or not. I've come to terms with the fact that I'm attracted to men, but haven't slept with a guy yet. I still haven't answered the question for myself of whether or not I'm actually gay.

VIII.

RISE OF THE RAGING 'MO

ANOTHER dark night evolves into another meaningless party. At least this time it has a fancy name to match all the suits we are wearing—*the Winter Formal*. Don't let the super clever name fool you into thinking it's anything more than just an excuse to try to introduce a bunch of boys-school boys to the opposite sex. Luckily this year we get the home field advantage, for anyone interested in going for goals. Not that anyone has much chance of scoring under the close supervision of priests and nuns armed to the teeth with rosaries and rulers. And I know from Sarah that some of them nuns are a crack shot with a piece of chalk. The annual event is intended to promote bonding with our sister school, but so far I haven't seen anything to support that.

Somewhere in the background Sarah hovers clear of me. She has been an angel of a sister since I told my family about my sexuality. She has been kind enough not to mention that small fact to Sandra either; who I'm also sure is lingering in the shadows somewhere. In fact, Sarah hasn't done anything to continue our sibling rivalry for a long time now. The sympathy card I apparently now hold for my inability to have children seems to have trumped her aces.

'Why must we do this thing every year?' Mark grumbles from his seat next to me.

'Huh?'

'I mean this formal is a complete waste of time. I could be out training or something more important. It's just an excuse for the girls to dress up and dance. It isn't really a guy thing.'

Despite his proclaimed objection to dressing up, Mark is looking utterly handsome this evening. He glows with the impression that his mother doused him in money to attract a daughter-in-law for her. The suit is dapper and subtly stylish. But for some reason Mark has shown absolutely no interest in the ten girls who have already plucked up the courage to ask him to dance, the others would be waiting for him to make the first move. Mark was quite content to just sit here with me. I was quite chuffed by the honour, and it provided the perfect vantage point to watch the peahens taking the role of their male counterpart in the animal world to flicker and fan their exquisite colors, perch their rears in direct view, only to be waved away by my silk-coated peacock seeking to hide his true beauty next to me in the shadows. At any event other than school or a dance Mark would flit around like a butterfly between the different groups of people ensuring that everyone has a good time and embraces each other as equals. These dances suck the exuberance out of Mark, leaving a husk of boredom and a low pitched grumble.

'Some guys would think it's their thing,' I offer.

'Would that be um, your sort of guy?'

'Pfft, no. Just look at Bradley over there. He's really breaking down the moves.' And it appears, at risk of breaking his pants or someone's arm in the process. The rigid flailing limbs clearly identify him as a species on the brink of extinction. Nothing would want to mate with that, and all the others of his kind would have been slaughtered if they ventured too close.

'True,' Mark laughs. 'I think he's trying to get lucky but no girl can get close enough to him with those moves.'

'He does have a following though, look at all the guys pretending to dance around him.'

'They're just waiting for him to fall on his arse,' Mark adds. Formals really do bring out the harsher side of him. 'Speaking of arses, it looks like you are about to have yours kicked.' Mark nods in the direction of a charging bull. Sandra marches forward and plants herself directly in front of me.

'Can we have a word?' she asks, the politeness forced through clenched teeth.

'Um, I guess so,' I respond, easing gently from my seat, hands splayed to indicate I mean no harm. Mark's hand on my back firmly pushes me out of my seat and directly toward Sandra. Apparently he wants me to sort this out almost as much as Sandra. Sandra leads me away, taking a beeline to the main door and out into the crisp night air. The chill of her stare stings more than the cold breeze. Sandra stalks out to a dark patch along the side of the hall and snaps around on her heels.

'Who am I to you?' she demands, her rage vibrating clearly in the air even though her face is masked by the night.

'Um, Sandra?' I offer neutrally.

'What?'

'Sandra is who you are, and it's the same for me as it would be for anyone else.'

'Is that all?'

'What do you mean?'

'Am I just Sandra to you? Nothing more than that? Is that why you refused to do more than have sex with me? I'm just Sandra?'

'Wait, what? Why are you lining me up like this? You made a move on me, and then ran away. I don't remember anything more being offered.'

'It was later but you refused. Why?'

'Why what?'

'Why did you refuse me? You only want sex from girls, is that it?'

I can't help but feel these lines were carefully extracted from a late afternoon soap opera.

'I refused,' I begin to answer, pausing to choose my words carefully. 'I refused because I can't have anything more with you.'

'There's someone else? I was the other girl?' Her hands fly around as if they have a mind of their own, the illusion eerily similar to the snakes whipping out from Medusa's head. My words were obviously not what she wanted to hear.

'No there isn't someone else. I'm just not in the position to be in any relationships at the moment. I've got a lot on my plate and don't want to commit to something that

I couldn't be fully into because of my current situation.' There, that should stump her for now and it appears to have worked well. Sandra is quiet, pondering my statement. Her shadow lies menacingly still, bordering on a second wave of attack.

'So it has nothing to do with me?'

'No,' I produce the kindest voice I can manage.

'Then why would your sister give me your number? She made it sound as if there might be something in it and then like an idiot I got carried away. I'm not usually like this. I don't usually get so attached, it's just we had a great night, you're nice and I thought I would go out on a limb.'

'I don't know why Sarah would encourage it. I've never talked with her about it. She was just meddling, I guess.'

'But I'm definitely not the reason you can't go out with me?'

'Definitely. It was nothing that you did or didn't do. It's all me.'

Sandra's rage deflates with this offering. Her ego remains intact, except for the displays of tears and tantrums, but as far as I know that's common for girls her age anyway. Sarah is prone tears at the drop of a hat.

'Are you sure?'

'Yes. I don't think I could be surer of anything.'

'Oh, okay. Well, I'm sorry to seek you out like that. I guess next time I'll have to make sure I understand the situation before letting my imagination jump into something.'

'Yeah, possibly.'

'Okay, well, I'll see you around then.' Sandra glides directly towards the hall to avoid further conversation. I'm glad she has disappeared now. I was creeping along hot coals as it was with that conversation, where one foot wrong would threaten to engulf me in fire. I take the time to meander for a lap around the hall alone to clear my head of all this nonsense, especially Sandra's attachment issues. I'm glad to see she's not crazy though.

'That was awkward,' a voice fires out from the dark. I jolt in surprise. 'Sorry mate, I didn't want to interrupt the two of you, and you managed to talk your way out of copping the brunt of her anger.'

'That doesn't mean you couldn't try to save me from it,' I joke, hoping the shock of company doesn't show in my wavering voice.

'Nah, I think you handled it well,' the voice becomes familiar. A shadow grows out from beneath the tree, broad shoulders and stiff hips outlining his masculinity. I calm more when I recognise it's Thomas, the brooding muso from my geography class.

'Cheers. What were you doing out here anyway? And by yourself?'

'I had to get away, all the music and girls screaming. Not my cup of tea. I get it enough at home with two sisters. I don't need it here on a night out.'

'That's fair enough. Have you been out here long?'

'Ten minutes maybe. I was planning on walking around the oval to kill some time, stopped to turn the tree into a toilet and then your argument began. Was that the girl everyone says you slept with?'

'Yeah,' I groan. 'I think that's going to haunt me forever. I can't go back in there right now and deal with all the questions.'

'To the oval?' Thomas offers.

'Sounds like a plan to me.'

As with anything in this school, the walk to the oval is anything but straightforward. A maze of corridors and cloisters combined with a random array of locked passages turns the stroll to the other side of the school into a labyrinth of complex proportions. We duck and weave through the available corridors, our footsteps echoing into the distance, our suits providing enough warmth to hold the cold at bay. We make it to the oval to find it more deserted than the buildings, as though the formal was a magnet sucking in all the corsages and cufflinks to a single point away from us.

'This place is eerie,' Thomas says as we arrive at the darkened grandstand. 'I thought at night there were always lights on to keep the students away.'

'Not much point tonight if all the students are at the Winter Formal.'

'Yeah, I reckon,' he sighs. 'I can't believe so much time and effort has gone into the dance this year.'

'Not as much as last year. We had dance lessons, practicing with each other.' I can sense Thomas shudder as we walk next to each other around the oval. 'Exactly. I was always too confused about who the guy was and who the girl was. They must have thought we all remember the formal dances from last year.'

'Not if you're new this year. You're thrown in with the sharks then.'

'True, true. They were rather feisty this year,' I say.

'Yeah, speaking of which, what's with you and that Sandra girl? Everyone said that you got it on?'

'Well, yeah… we did, but only once, and there's nothing more to say about it.'

'Really? But what was it like?'

'Huh?'

'You know,' he whispers as if someone is waiting to pounce at the mention of something taboo. 'Sex.'

'Oh, that. It was okay.'

'Okay? Is that it?'

'Yeah.'

'What did she do?'

'Why do you want to know all this?'

'I don't know. I just thought I'd ask while I have the chance. Most of the guys around school only pretend to have had sex so they can't really tell anyone anything about it. It doesn't sound like it's much to write home about, yet all those douches brag about what they did and how awesome it is.'

'And how awesome they were at it.'

We round the bend of the oval and arrive back at the edge of the grandstand. Mindlessly we stroll up the steps to the patch of shadows in the back, usually where all the so-called 'druggies' like to hang out. Thomas peers into the darkness ensuring there's nothing poking out he might sit on—needles that is. He collapses onto the seat at the back and loosens his tie, glancing over each shoulder and over the edge of the grandstand before talking again.

'So, who started it?' he speaks a little more confidently now he can guarantee we're alone.

'Started what?' I pretend to be unaware he's still on that topic of conversation. I plant myself down near to Thomas, the crash of my arse on the seat an attempt to signal that a real man is sitting down, beware. The metallic seating echoes as we sit, ringing out into the empty night. We could turn them into a drum set without attracting the attention of anyone at the school.

'Who made the first move? Did Sandra hit on you? Or did you go for it?'

'Oh, she did. We were in the parents' bedroom at the party and she made the first move on me.'

'How? I heard a rumour that she put porn on to try and get you randy before going down on you. I also heard that you started the porn and she slapped you when you said you didn't have a condom.'

'Really? That's great. I'm surprised at how detailed the stories are considering only the two people who were there would know how it went.'

'Exactly, you can't trust anyone. So how did it go? She started it?'

I concede defeat, thinking there is no harm in letting Thomas know. We've known each other for years now and besides, no one would have any reason to believe him any more than anyone else. It would only throw another log onto the already burning rumour fire.

'She did make the first move,' I begin, 'and the part about her suggesting porn is right. I don't know if it was to get me horny or anything like that. I think it was just for fun.'

'She watches porn for fun? I didn't think girls liked porn.'

'Neither did I, but she knew where it was and we started watching it. It definitely was for a bit of fun from what I remember. We were sick of the beer so we ducked upstairs to get into the parents' stash of booze. Made cocktails and chilled out on the bed.'

'Was that before or after she started hitting on you?'

'Before. Or perhaps she was hitting on me from the start. Anyway, we'd finished our drinks before anything happened. We were just chatting, getting to know each other a little bit and then the porn went on and after a while she climbed on top of me and we started making out. From then one thing led to another and before I knew it we were having sex. There were condoms in the drawer next to the bed so we used one of them.'

'Awesome, what position were you in?'

'Missionary, nothing too exciting. It seemed to be the easier angle for us to do it the first time. It's what came natural to us.'

Thomas shifted uncomfortably, his hand pressing deeply into his crotch.

'Are you okay?' I ask.

'Um, yeah fine,' Thomas shudders out.

He's hard, I think instantly to myself. I'm a guy, I recognise that awkward shift to reposition an erection to hide the tell-tale outline. Up a little and to the side, that's where it goes. Thomas is flying the flag that all men have—the flag pole straight up and ready to pierce the sky. Even in the darkness his embarrassed shuffle across the metal seat is a clear signal.

'Are you sure you're okay?' I ask again. This is possibly one of the most awkward situations I've been in, and I've had sex with a girl. Once again that situation has led into something out of the ordinary. Is it rude to point out the obviousness of what's going on? Could that actually break the tension or would I be outing myself in the process? Should I sit closer, rub his back and let him know it's a completely natural process that all young men experience? What do I do? And to add to my confusion, I'm starting to become aroused too. The urge to scream out for an adjudicator tingles on the tip of my tongue, ready to be bellowed into the night. I know there should be no one nearby who can assist, but the temptation to yell out my confusion is almost irresistible.

'Yeah, fine,' he squirms. Surely his discomfort would decrease the growth in his pants, but it only seems to add to the rise.

'You're hard aren't you?' I blurt out.

He's startled for a moment but doesn't react straight away, questioning his next move. He decides to nod, a little sheepishly. It's endearing.

'Okay, that's fine,' I recover a little and try to comfort him. 'Would you like me to continue with what happened with Sandra?'

'What? Why would you?'

'You asked, and you are clearly enjoying it on some level. Now that the awkwardness is out in the open I thought you might want to hear some more, so we might as well finish? If not we could talk about something else. The sporting carnival is coming up again soon.'

'No, that's stupid. You hate sports and so do I. No, the story about Sandra is good. Everything else would just sound sexual now anyway, so we may as well talk about sex.'

'What do you want to hear next?'

'What was it like when you guys came?' He eases closer, listening intently.

'She went first. All the muscles inside of her tensed on my cock like nothing I've ever felt before. That's what made me blow.'

'Inside of her?'

'Yeah, almost the exact same time.'

'Cool,' he says, sliding more toward me. I freeze in shock at the sudden unexpected contact with another male. It's barely a tango between the hairs on our hands but enough to be obvious to the both of us. 'Then what happened?'

'Um,' I stutter, distracted by his closeness, wondering why he doesn't pull away. He would have to be ignoring the hand. I'm frozen, not wanting to pull back, too scared to push forward. How can he not know how close our hands are? The answer comes soon enough. I stumble over my reply while looking toward his eyes. They stare intently back, hanging off my every word, every movement pulsating in time to my heartbeat.

He leans in first, landing just to the side of my lips. I twitch in surprise. His lips explore their way across, sliding to line up with mine. We freeze, locked in a motionless kiss. I'm too stunned to know what to do, but Thomas waves the awkwardness out of the air and takes control. His lips part gently to allow his tongue passage. It flicks playfully around my lips, a sensual lubrication to ease its entrance into my mouth. The tongue dances about between my teeth, the sensation slapping its way down my spine. Thomas doesn't waste a moment, snatching my hand towards his crotch to show just how hard he was during my story. The erection fights against the fabric of his suit, pulsating beneath my fingers. My own cock stirs and straightens into launching position, much quicker than it had during my last intimate interaction. I feel like we've crossed a point of no return, not that I have any interest in backing out now. I latch my grip onto the back of Thomas' head and pull him deeper into the kiss. He moans deep from his chest. I fall backward onto the seat, dragging him on top as I move. Thomas responds without objection and slips eagerly into a position between my legs, pressing our hardness together.

My mind pounds with excitement. Every touch, every

breath blankets my body with pleasure. At the fall of each stroke every part of me pushes back for more. Nothing has felt more right than this. Nothing has run through me so naturally. Thomas reacts to my movements, and I to his. I lock my eyes onto his face as it twists into an expression of uncontrolled pleasure, and possibly pain, in the dim light.

I'm excited by the way Thomas takes charge despite his clumsy efforts. His fingers fumble at our pants, jolting and shaking until the zips release our straining erections. Presented with a penis now free for consumption, I'm eager to taste hard flesh pressed against my tongue, warm and salty-sweet. My amateur technique proves effective once I realise the dangers of teeth, and Thomas groans and tangles his fingers in my hair. He takes over again, easing me onto my back and mimicking the movements down my cock. Every stroke fires fresh nerves through my body, the sensation overwhelming and impossible to resist.

In a single sudden movement Thomas reunites our lips, his hand latching on to both erections. As his frantic tugs press his moist cock against mine, I feel the moment coming. The pleasure peaks in the feisty pounding of his hand down our cocks. With a final shudder and jerk, we cum. The droplets sprinkle like a warm sticky rain on my suit. Thomas releases a sigh, and then settles on top of me for a moment, breathless and silent. The warm comfort of the afterglow is cut short as reality claws its way back in, dragging awkwardness with it. Self-consciously we readjust ourselves and return to sitting next to each other.

As the lust drains away I find I'm drawn to more practical concerns. I'm relieved to find all the semen ended up on my shirt and can be hidden by my jacket. Once I'm sure the stains are something I can deal with later, my next problem is to relieve the awkwardness. I want to break the silence before it gets too uncomfortable, shatter it into a billion tiny pieces so we can plan our next move in this situation. For me it all felt right. The process of intimacy between myself and another guy was more natural than the sun rising. Even without penetration, the sex with Thomas was still more thrilling and mind-blowing, felt more complete and real, than the brief time spent with Sandra.

'So,' I interject into the quiet.

'So,' he answers, his mind apparently blank of thoughts as well. This brief interaction isn't enough for me. I want to let Thomas know what this meant for me, that everything was going to be okay. But I was struggling to find the words, and while I was distracted searching for the right ones, something else popped out.

'You're gay then?'

'NO!' Thomas snaps. Damnit, it wasn't the cleverest thing for me to say. I don't dare try saying anything else, and Thomas leaps into the silence. 'Well, I don't think I am. I've never done anything like that before. I've really never even thought about it before. I um… I gotta go.' He jumps up from his seat as if to make good his escape from some terrible danger. Suddenly he twists around, finger shaking desperately as me. 'Can we not tell anyone about this, please?' his voice tremulous and pleading.

'Sure, we don't have to tell anyone about it. But if you ever need to talk, I can be available.'

'I don't think so, I'm fine,' he pauses before offering a final, 'thank you.' Then he's gone, his shadow absorbed into the night.

I remain planted to the seat, unwilling to move until my mind works through the situation. I have now had sex (of a sort) with a guy, and there was nothing wrong about it. It was quite thrilling actually, more powerful and overwhelming than I expected. I don't think there could be a better way to confirm you sexual identity than experiencing it first-hand like that. I was always aware of it, but this whacks on a big stamp of approval, confirming exactly what I have been feeling all along. It was so right. Nothing could tell me otherwise. This is the only justification I need of who I am and what I like. The justification of what feels natural for me.

IX

A CROWD

'Thomas,' Mark stutters in complete disbelief. 'Thomas MacArthur?'

'Yep,' I nod, avoiding eye contact as we sit next to each other at the tennis courts.

'Thomas?'

'Yep.'

Weeks have passed since the formal, yet I have only just released the information to Mark. I'd tried my best to honour my promise of secrecy to Thomas, but keeping information from Mark was just burning me up inside. Especially since Thomas had approached me earlier today asking to catch up again sometime and it wasn't to talk. I assume there would be talking involved but that didn't appear to be the primary reason for catching up. Well, that's not the impression that I got from him, anyway. He'd spoken in a hushed tone, eyes darting furtively around the corridor to ensure no one was watching (or at least not judging) as he asked me to come over to his house after school. The scene flashed in my head again like a grizzly accident.

'Me and a mate are thinking of a bit of sport,' Thomas ended, his voice returning to normal volume to make clear he was talking about a safe, masculine activity.

'Um, sure I guess,' I answered thoughtlessly, and to my detriment. I hadn't thought the entire conversation through. I just wanted it to end. The 'mate' part hadn't even registered on my radar. I assume it was just Thomas not wanting anyone to think it is only us catching up, but I couldn't be sure.

'You're becoming a sex fiend,' Mark mocks.

'Shut up. It's only been two people.'

'Yeah, and they both keep coming back for more. Does being gay give you special sexual powers?'

'Don't be stupid.'

'I wonder what I would be like if I was gay,' Mark ponders, his face textured with creative concentration. 'I don't think I'd be that fantastic in bed.'

'You haven't had sex yet to know.'

'I know. I just don't know what to do.'

'Think of it as sport. It's just like tackling someone, but with extra bits.'

'Ha, I really don't think I could approach it like a normal tackle,' he laughs. 'But I still think I wouldn't make a good gay man.'

'Yeah, because there's just one set definition of what a gay man's supposed to be like,' I lay my sarcasm on thick, to make sure Mark gets it.

'Well, you know. Most gay people flaunt it. They're gay and they want the world to know it. It's almost as if they have only one defining feature and that's their sexuality. I wouldn't fit that categorisation of gay.'

'Like me, you mean?'

Mark looks up guiltily. 'I know you're not that kind of gay, but you're different.'

'How so?'

'I guess it's just that I know you. I know you're normal. But other gays are just gay.'

I laugh. 'I'm normal. I like how you use that word.'

Mark shifts uncomfortably on the seat. 'You know what I mean.'

'Maybe, but it might be nice if you could say what you mean.'

'It's just, I'm not comfortable flaunting my sexuality about all the time, gay or straight, so I don't like it when other people do the same,' he explains.

I must admit this is true, I don't recall a situation where Mark's sexuality has ever been visible. Of course his broad shoulders and athletic prowess outweigh any notion he might be anything other than straight. Mark is bright enough to know that I won't let his choice of words go easily, so he seeks to distract me with further questions.

'So what are you going to do about Thomas?'

'I don't know,' I reply, deciding to let him off for the moment. 'I think I need to talk to someone about this.'

'Well, you're talking to me.'

'Yeah, and I appreciate it. But I need some insight from someone who knows more about these things than we do. I don't know if I should break it off or just go with the flow. And if I do break it off, I need to work out how to do it. I didn't do so well with Sandra.'

'So, will you talk to your parents then? Or maybe Father D?'

'Yeah, I'm really not ready to talk about boys with my parents yet. But Father Donovan has been good to talk to before, so I'll probably try him. You know, I really didn't expect a priest to deal with this very well, but he's been pretty fantastic really. I reckon he knows more than he lets on.'

'I know,' Mark agrees, 'I think he must have had a really radical life before becoming a priest.'

'I don't think it works like that. You have to study for ages to be ordained.'

'I know, I know. But I still get a weird vibe when I'm with him,' Mark shivers.

'What, you don't like him?'

'No, no, it's not that. I just feel weird when I'm too close to him. It's as if he's judging me. No, more like assessing me. And there's something he's hiding. I feel like he's watching me in a bad way.'

'In a pedo way?'

'Yeah, but I don't think he's a pedo. They wouldn't allow people like that in the church.' (Oh, poor naïve, trusting Mark.)

'That's bizarre. I've never had that feeling from him,' I say.

'You've never felt like he's hiding something or too interested in what the guys here do?'

'No, I always thought that was just his job. He's supposed to be a guidance counsellor. He's supposed to show interest and know a lot about the students here. But I do feel a little weird sometimes. He stares as if he knows something we don't, but then he does seem to know everyone's secrets too. He probably even knows secrets about our parents. He's been at the school for long enough.'

'I suppose you're right. I just get a weird vibe from him.'

I decide to wait until the end of lunch before I go to see Father Donovan, because I start to feel like my issues aren't a big deal, and there might be others with more pressing problems. But Mark's 'weird vibe' sticks in my head right up until I walk into Father Donovan's office. It's amazing how quickly that seed of doubt takes hold—I'd never even had the slightest concern about Father Donovan before, but now despite knowing him for many years, despite all the help he's given me and other students, and despite that never once has anyone ever spoken against him, it's now hard to dismiss the ghostly presence of doubt that threatens to pounce at any given second.

'Come on in,' Father Donovan welcomes me into his office with the usual benign cheer.

'Thank you,' I say, settling uncomfortably into the seat opposite Father Donovan.

'What can I do for you today?'

'Well,' my mind races on where I should begin. *I screwed a guy, he wants more, I'm a raging, hormonally driven maniac, can you forgive me? What would Jesus do?* 'I have a situation happening with a guy at school and I need some advice on what to do.'

'Oh,' Father Donovan leans in to provide his full attention. His eyes gleam with anticipation. Maybe Mark is right, maybe there is a slither of paedophilia wafting through Father Donovan's veins. Father Donovan may have leaned forward to show interest at every other meeting, but only now do I feel somewhat uncomfortable with the gesture. 'And by situation you mean...?'

'Um,' I stare back at him. His right eye twitches, a blur to any onlooker but still a noticeable tic. I've never seen it before. Does this topic excite him to the point that his eye twitches with lustful anticipation. I know it's ridiculous, but I can't think of any other way to explain the sudden eye movement. 'Kinda sexual,' I finish the sentence, unwilling to let the eye scare me into silence.

'I see. Do you have more questions about understanding the nature of your sexuality, or about the Catholic view of it?'

'Just sexuality this time, too much has been happening for me to really focus on managing the religious side of my life at the moment.'

'My young man, faith isn't something for you to manage or deal with. Faith is what helps you to deal with everything else. The opportunities to embrace forgiveness and faith are everywhere, the challenge is to face these opportunities rather than fall victim to them.'

'Okay, I'll try to, I guess. Like I said I haven't really thought through it all.'

'Fair enough, the life of a busy teenager. So tell me, what's the current situation,' his right eye quivers again.

'It's a situation with another guy. Something happened between us. It sort of just happened without me meaning it to, and now he has invited me around to his house and I'm not sure what I should do.'

'What do you want to do?'

'Other than hide away and pretend it never happened?'

'Yes exactly, what is your heart telling you?'

'Um… I think my heart is curious. It wants to know what's happening and what the guy is after.'

'And what are you after?'

'I think I'm open to the opportunity. I'm a little curious myself. I want to know what else is going to happen now. It was my first time with a guy and it was good. I wouldn't mind exploring further, and it's probably best to be with the one guy rather than many,' I reveal to Father Donovan, blurting it all out without thinking.

I think I've just convinced myself to meet Thomas again. It was an exciting experience. My spine (and another appendage) tingles with the memories of our short tryst together in the grandstand, and I'm sure that was only the beginning. There's so much more on offer in being with a guy. A sexual awakening awaits my arrival.

'So go through with it. Catch up with him,' Father Donovan prompts. 'But always, absolutely always, remember to be safe. If at any point you feel uncomfortable, even if you are just chatting with someone, I can't tell you how many times I have stressed this with the students here, if in any situation, at home, with friends, with others in your life, if you are uncomfortable, stop. No questions about it. Stop. You have every right to stop something you are not comfortable with. It is the same as bullying at school. People are uncomfortable with it and can generally do something about it to make it stop.'

'Wow, thank you. I didn't think you would be so understanding,' I half lie, half acknowledge I'm actually stunned by a priest who accepts difference in people, including the gay one. 'I'm just doing my job,' Father Donovan says. 'Once again, it's probably time you go for class or you'll be late.'

'Thank you,' I repeat and duck out of his office.

* * *

The decision has been made. I stand out the front of Thomas' house, and find myself glued to the pavement. I've managed to walk the entire way without contemplating what's waiting on the other side of that door, but now that I'm confronted with it thoughts stampede through my brain, rampant hooves throwing up images of gay orgies, piñatas, bible study… a herd of possibilities to trample any attempt at common sense.

I inhale slowly to soothe my nervousness. *Make this easier*, I pray silently. It isn't a complex task in any way, but lifting my finger to the doorbell requires all my concentration. Raise one digit, point in the direction of the cheap plastic fixture, press inwards, listen for the *ding dong* in the distance, await the resident to open the front door. As I wait I distract myself with pointless observations. *This house hasn't changed much from how I remember it, the peeling grey paint that hangs from the overfull gutters really adds to the charm, have they really done no maintenance at all in the six years since I was here for Thomas' 10th birthday?*

The door yanks open and startles me from my musings, and to my shame I jump and let out a squeal while my hands flap like a saloon door. Great, screaming at a door that I knew was going to open was not the masculine arrival I had hoped for. Thomas laughs nervously.

'How's that for timing,' he said.

'Yeah, almost too good,' I play along, ignoring the fact I've been here for a good ten minutes.

Thomas shifts uncomfortably on his feet.

'So, um, what do you want to do?' he asks, his eyes staring off into the distance to ignore facing me directly.

'What do you mean?' I answer back. 'This was your idea.'

'Oh, yeah, right. I forgot.' He stumbles over his words as if unsettled by my mere presence. Shouldn't he know what he wanted to do? This was all his idea. I just happened to be curious enough to come along for the ride. 'I was wondering… well, thinking more so than anything, that we could, maybe… it all depends on what you want to do I mean… there's no pressure to do anything either way, I was just wondering.' I nod blankly waiting for an actual question to emerge, at this point anything plausible and coherent would do. Nerves are throwing me off balance, his nerves even more so. I would answer yes to anything just for this awkwardness to pass. 'Would you like to go to the movies or something?' he finally offers. *Or something?* That could be anything. Oh, how the mind could charge away on a journey with that thought. I rein my brain in before it gets too far, and play dumb just to see how far Thomas would get by himself.

'Um, what?'

'You know, an um… you know, date or something?'

'Ah,' I let myself breathe again. 'You're asking me out.' He nods. 'But I thought you weren't gay.'

'I'm not,' he snaps instantly. A look of regret rose quickly on his face. 'I'm sorry. I mean I don't think I am, but in the grandstand I had a good time and now I'm completely confused about what to do.'

'So asking me out is the next step?'

'I don't know. I've never done this before. Not even with a girl. In my head it sounded like the right thing to do. You fool around with someone, and then you should date them. At least give it a go.'

It sounded reasonable to me, in some sense. Except it hadn't been reason enough for me.

'So why did I have to come around here for you to ask me out? You couldn't have done it at school or texted me.'

Thomas snorts. 'No way in hell. I could be busted at school and even if I did have your number I wasn't going to leave a trail for someone to find.'

His paranoia might have been amusing if I hadn't recently experienced the exact same feelings myself. I hold onto my thoughts for a moment to weigh up my options, all of which point towards very little, other than time, which could be wasted by going on a date. And if the movie is an incredible blockbuster it would be time well spent.

'A movie sounds great,' I say. I pause for a moment before I broach the next dilemma. Not the choice in movie, that one comes later. 'What if people see us together?'

'It's not like I'll be holding your hand or anything. We're just mates hanging out.' *Just mates. How boring.* 'So, ready to go? I have a car for the rest of the evening.'

'You have a car?' I like the sound of this.

'Well, its mum's. She works nearby so only drives when it's raining. Don't you drive your parents' car?'

'Nah, I don't even have a license—never needed it. I take the bus if I need to get anywhere.'

'No worries. I can get us there. I'll just grab the keys.'

It isn't long before we are cruising along the streets in a neat little pink number with all the trimmings. That description would sound reasonable for a bridesmaid dress, but this is a car. Fluff lines every patch of interior. Little loose bits of frill tickle the back of my ears. Stuffed dice (more pink fur) dangle wildly from the rear vision mirror while dogs bob their heads at us from the dashboard. Thomas flushed red as soon as he pulled out of the driveway. I hold back the chuckles at the most spectacularly impractical car I've ever seen.

'Dad has the wagon,' Thomas attempts in justification. 'This is just mum's car to get around town. I thought my 'rents were buying a car for all of us when I got my license, you know, a manual for me to learn to drive, and this is what they brought back.'

It quickly makes sense. What better way to deter your teenage son from hoon driving than making him drive a car that is *obviously* not his, and certainly not one he'd want to draw attention to. Most of the guys at school would hate the thought of a speed camera, or their friends, snapping a photo of them in this little beast. Thomas falls silent as we approach the cinema, and he shrinks further into his seat. Shivers spasm through his hands as he crunches between gears and sneaks around bends. Internally, I judge him, though mainly to avoid my own quaking thoughts. And it's not even the prospect of being seen in a hot pink car that's on my mind. I'm just totally mentally unprepared for today to be the day that I go on my first date. I'd considered the possibility that sex was a potential outcome, but not an actual date. Too many thoughts and scenarios scream through my head on repeat. I steel my mind as best I can against the mutiny in my brain and try to focus on the guy driving me out to the movies. He's playing down his usual muso façade this evening. He polishes up nicely with his hair flattened down rather than spiked in all directions. The basic jeans and shirt combo adds a nice touch to his ribbed physique, though at the wrong angle it could look like he needs a good feed. Strange, those thin lips of his I kissed not so long ago are not as tantalising in the light as they were in the dark.

It comes as no surprise when Thomas parks five minutes away from the cinema in a little cul-de-sac with little chance of one of our schoolmates happening past. The long shadows struck by sun behind the trees and hedges lining the secluded street would make a perfect spot for a drug deal. Or as the case may be, a gay date. I hadn't expected my first date to feel so shady and illicit.

Thomas slides wordlessly out of the car and leads the way down the few streets to the cinema complex. He hands remain shoved firmly inside his pockets while his eyes dart around to probe every lurking shadow. A laugh hisses out from between my lips—his attempt to hide himself is so comically obvious I couldn't hold it in any longer.

'What are you doing?' I ask.

'Huh?' he looks back at me. 'I'm just making sure we aren't seen by anyone.'

'And the best way is to shift around suspiciously? You look like you are about to rob a bank for the first time.' I laugh nervously.

Thomas pauses for a second before nodding.

'You're right,' he says. 'We're just mates, hanging out.' He reaffirms to himself. He sucks in a deep breath and releases a huge soothing sigh. I'm glad he does, as I find I can relax more once he calms a little. Nerves are definitely contagious. *I hope it's the only thing I catch tonight,* I muse to myself as we round the corner to the cinema entrance.

'So, what do you wanna watch?' Thomas asks, staring at the session times.

'Anything with a bit of comedy would suit me.'

'Well… there only seems to be a romantic comedy on now, or kids' movies. Everything else won't start for a couple of hours, but I have to be home before then.'

Ha, even I know that's a rookie move—*It's not that I'm not having fun but I have to get home now*—would be a perfect excuse to escape a bad date, but he's blown that now.

'The romcom it is then.'

Thomas heads off to purchase the tickets without a chance of protest from me. So far so good—I'm glad he's decided to be the gentleman so that I don't have to be. Also, I don't do queues.

'OH MY GOD,' a squeal pierces the air from twenty metres away. As I turn to confront the shriek I spot Daniel charging forward, hands flailing excitedly. 'What are you doing here?' he says throwing his arms around me in a tight squeeze. I freeze. He's never touched me before, let alone hugged me.

'Um…' is all I can stutter until he releases me. 'I'm here to watch a movie with a friend.'

'Ha, you have friends? Pull the other one.' I stare blankly, unimpressed. 'Oh, you actually mean it. Here I was thinking you might be on a date with that girl I helped you with. So where is this lucky friend?'

'He… he's buying tickets now.'

'Tickets? Plural? Well someone's keen aren't they? It seems you *are* on a date after all.'

Before I can protest, Daniel spins around to identify his target for interrogation. I'm not convinced he actually does think I'm on a date, and I try on my best nonchalant face to throw him off the scent. He probably just wants to confirm that I do in fact have friends. His hunt doesn't last long. Thomas turns from the ticket counter and after a few steps halts instantly. His eyes glaze over as his face solidifies into a look of guilt and panic. But behind it I can see the cogs whirring in his head, piecing together the tableau of Daniel and I staring at him. He reminds me of nothing so much as a kangaroo frozen in oncoming headlights, hoping against hope that stillness will save him from the hurtling semi-trailer that is the full force of Daniel's personality.

'I'm Daniel.' The lisping introduction is accompanied by a sashay and a hand thrust forward.

'Um yeah, I'm Thomas,' comes the stumbling reply, though he doesn't move, or even look at the outstretched hand. Daniel's laughter bubbles forth.

'I'm not that scary,' he cries, in the face of all the evidence.

Thomas hesitates for a moment longer before rallying with his butchest reply and taking Daniel's hand. 'Yeah, good to meet you mate.'

'Come on Thomas, firm it up,' Daniel chides enthu-siastically. 'Nothing worse than a dead fish handshake. So, how do you guys know each other?'

Thomas hesitates again, thrown by his attempt at masculinity failing through poor delivery. I can see he's coming to understand that acting like we're mates is harder than he first planned, and jump in to rescue him. I have an advantage here, knowing how to manage Daniel.

'We go to school together,' I say as if it is nothing at all.

'Well where are the rest of your mates? Anyone would see just the two of you and think you're on a date,' Daniel teases. The blood drains from Thomas' cheeks.

'Dude, that's not cool. Thomas hasn't worked it out yet, and if you're not careful you'll scare him off. Cock-block me and it won't end well for you,' I try to joke, possibly taking it a little too far, but that's how you need to handle Daniel. Thomas though, begins to sway. Daniel lets out a typical over-the-top laugh, drawing the eyes of passersby.

'Yeah good one, breeder,' Daniel laughs. 'You're too straight to be gay.'

'Well, now I'm just offended,' I fire back.

'Oh, let it go. So what movie are you seeing?'

Thomas, expression still blank, holds up our tickets.

'Oh… my… GOD!' Daniel shrieks again. I jolt from the noise—it's much harder to handle from close range. 'That's the same as me. I'm totally sitting with you guys.'

'Aren't you here with someone?' I try to ward him off.

'Not for lack of trying. I can't imagine why it's so hard to get someone to come with me, because Sarah Jessica Parker is so fabulous, but I decided to come by myself. But as fate would have it I'll have company anyway. Are you guys getting snacks first?'

'Nah, I'm all good,' I answer. Thomas simply shakes his head.

'Great, let's go,' Daniel says slipping his arm inside

Thomas' and leading him toward our cinema. I choke back the laughter at his flurry of expressions. Clearly he hasn't encountered a confidently open gay man and suddenly there's one latched onto his arm ready to canoodle with him. All Thomas can manage is a small quiver of his lip in protest as he is marched into the dark enclosure of the cinema. I'm tickled by the hilarious irony—Thomas, who hides any hint at gayness behind excessive masculinity, has been overpowered by Daniel's confidence and willingness to openly brush up against another guy. By sheer coincidence I've offered up Thomas as fresh meat to Daniel. At least this would make working with him more bearable for another week or so.

As for our actual date, I do believe it has been hijacked. It's strange though, I don't feel any real disappointment. I didn't have any prior experience to have developed the slightest expectation about how it should all go. All the movie clichés, like asking my dad's permission beforehand, maybe bring me a gift to woo me, and then ending the night with a gentle embrace of our lips, just don't seem to fit here. For the first time, I wished there was some kind of role model within popular culture, just so I knew what to do.

The three of us snuggle into our seats toward the middle of the cinema. An elderly couple shuffles into the front row, avoiding the steps and giving us the only company we would have for this session. Apparently it's not a popular movie, or time of day. I guess most people would still be at work for another half an hour or so. Daniel still clings to Thomas' arm while prattling off into a one-sided conversation about his last week of work and shopping, in great depth, without forgetting a single detail. Poor Thomas is too stunned to comment, which is lucky for Daniel. Thomas' petrified glaze provides the perfect audience for Daniel to unleash every minute description about the coat he bought online for a bargain price. Thankfully years of working together has trained me to zone out when the ranting begins.

'You look tense,' Daniel says, snapping me out of my thoughts. 'You need to relax, I only bite on request.' Daniel latches on to the back of Thomas' neck and begins massaging away at the muscles. I have never seen him so quick to make physical contact with someone, and Thomas stiffens at the unexpected touch. To my surprise the shocked expression from Thomas soon dissipates into a dopey grin reminiscent of someone about to comfortably slip into a nanna nap. I don't believe it. Daniel's upfront and hands-on approach is working a charm.

'Oh, ah, that's so good,' Thomas moans.

'Shh!' the elderly gentleman shushes from in front of us. The trailers have barely started but I'm sure that moan wasn't what they wanted to hear. I instinctively hold myself back from commenting. Witty retorts are Daniel's territory, yet nothing comes from him.

Finally, the feature film flickers onto to the screen and the lights fade to leave us to join the shadows. I pray for more darkness. From the corner of my eye I see the proud and forthright words Daniel is whispering gently into Thomas' ear are casting a delightful spell on him. Who would have thought a blunt personality is what Thomas needs and falls for? I guess my quieter approach to expressing my sexuality didn't radiate enough confidence that Thomas could take on to feel comfortable and confident in his sexuality.

The movie couldn't end quickly enough for me. I've suddenly found myself to be a third wheel on my own date, and I don't want to impose for much longer. Just long enough to score a ride home again. As the lights come on I notice carefully placed hands slide away from Thomas' knee, where it must have been toying with leg hairs or something like that. I don't want to imagine what else they might have been doing next to me.

I clear my throat. 'Well, that was interesting,' I observe, though I'm not talking about the movie. 'I think I'm ready to head home, I'm starving and I'm expected back for dinner at some point.'

Without waiting to see if I'm followed I turn and lead the way from the cinema. I'm left waiting outside for what feels like half an hour, but was probably an impatient thirty seconds, before Thomas and Daniel emerge, Daniel cheekily typing away onto a cell phone as I tap my foot.

'Well, if you're in a flexible arrangement,' Daniel throws looks between Thomas and I. 'Then I'd love to catch up again sometime,' he says, returning Thomas' mobile.

'Sure that would be great,' Thomas replies. 'Maybe next weekend?'

'Sure thing. Let me know.' Daniel waves to both of us, spins and disappears quickly around a street corner.

It's a fair assessment that an analytical discussion of the ineffectiveness of the film's techniques to connect with an audience would not be the primary topic of conversation while Thomas drove me home. *Why wasn't I already dating Daniel? He sounds like so much fun. I didn't know you knew many gay people. I just felt so great listening to him. I think I'm definitely attracted to him.* These were the words spewing out from Thomas' lips. I barely give a stiff nod in response and he whirls into another spiel about my co-worker's greatness. I would be very happy for Thomas to meet someone that makes him shine the way he is now, but I'd rather this date end immediately and then begin congratulating Thomas on his newfound glory a bit later, when I wasn't feeling so shit about myself.

Eventually, Thomas picked up on this.

'I'm terribly sorry about how things went,' Thomas tries as I jump out of the car.

'No, that's perfectly fine,' I dismiss, wishing I had the guts to say it really wasn't. 'We were just mates hanging out.'

'Yeah, you're right,' Thomas nods absent mindlessly. 'Just mates. I wonder what'll happen with Daniel and me.'

'No need to wait, just text him when you get home. Off you go,' I encourage.

'You know, you're right. Okay, seeya,' he says, pulling away from the curb.

'Yep, bye,' I wave. *Thank God that's over.*

X.

THE CLOSET IS FOR CLOTHES AND CHRISTMAS PRESENTS

JESUS haunts me. Weeks pass into the season of new growth and he's been following my footsteps doggedly. I'm not sure whether it's due to his influence or I'm just unlucky, but I haven't had any further confirmation of my sexuality since Thomas. So yeah, I can have sex with another guy, but is that enough to be gay? Could I spend the rest of my life with another guy? Could I *love* a guy... actually be in love with him? These are the questions buzzing inside my head, and I can't get any clarity on these things.

I had wanted to talk about it with Thomas—finally I thought I'd found someone who shared my experiences, who would understand. But even though he's dating Daniel now, I think he'd rather I not mention it or our failed date. And I swear I've already heard more about it than I can handle from Daniel—he's never shy on those details. I squirm just thinking about some of them. It's a lot easier at work now that Daniel is flying high on the essence of a new love. But even so, my own conscience (or the looming spectre of Jesus, or whatever it is) has been bugging me. I've gone against the teachings of the church and my good Christian upbringing to follow my heart and take the path that feels natural for me.

This confusion is a blessing and a curse. It encourages introspection and spurs me to ask questions, and sometimes I come away understanding who I am and the direction I'm heading a little bit better. At other times it opens up a well of self-doubt, which undermines all the work I've done to know myself and slowly beats me down to a fizzling anxious mess, all of my confidence and self-esteem evaporated to nothing. So far all the experiences I've had with sharing this part of myself—with family, my closest friend even the school chaplain have been positive and accepting, without requiring any change from me. Yet, the lingering conflict with my faith sneaks up behind me and jabs me in the ribs each time I look around a corner, thinking my path is clear. I need to release myself of this. I need to be able to know that I'll be accepted into heaven like any other member of my faith rather than be forced into hell for who I am.

If only the next step towards that was easy, or even clear. What do I search for? Social acceptance? Religious acceptance? Emotional acceptance? And who do I want acceptance from? Other people, the world, or just myself? Do I really love and embrace myself enough? Am I to scream from the rooftops that I'm fine with who I am and anyone who can't accept it can get stuffed?

With so much to think about it's difficult to focus on the speech on the reproduction of Shakespeare in modern times for English class. Under different circumstances I'd think it was an interesting topic, if it wasn't perfectly destroyed by Roger as he stutters through his presentation, a nervous wreck in front of the whole class. I don't think he knows that we're all more concerned with the discomfort of our own hot, sweaty bodies. Who knows why Mr Simons refuses to switch on the air conditioning? He might be a secret hippie, someone who doesn't want to burn more fossil fuels than he needs to.

'So like, nothing we do these days is ever original,' Roger ventures into his conclusion. 'Shakespeare did it all. He was the real modernist. He created everything we do today but it's so, like, mixed into our society that we don't even know it's there. So I leave you with this thought, is anything you've done really original?'

We clap politely, more out of habit than for his C+ performance. Roger has never been the brightest spark but he always gives it a fair go.

'That was painful,' I murmur.

'Wasn't too bad,' Mark defends him.

Mr Simons adjusts his beard and skulks to the front of the class. The teaching salary must be that good to bring this wilderness lover in from the wild for the semester. An image of him logging his way through a forest jumps to mind and entertains me for the brief second before he starts talking.

'That was slightly off topic Roger. Yes, he was a fantastic creator and modern for his time, but he too would have had influences in his writing. It's the same with Dante and his Divine Comedy with the main character of Virgil, his inspiration. Let's see if we can keep a little more on track with the next presentation.' He calls my name. 'Let's see how the writing of Shakespeare has assisted with your presentation.'

I'd prepared for the speech, at some point in time that now seems like the distant past, but was too distracted with worry about the damnation of my eternal soul to concentrate on getting myself in the right headspace for speaking in front of people. I slide out of my seat, gathering my notes as I do. The small squares of card sit like cement slabs in my hand. They have everything I need; containing a summary of the points I want to make and weighing down my wrist to hide the shaking. I feel like I'm barely present, but the scribbled hints provide a nudge in the back to spill everything I know about Shakespeare and his conversion from comedy to pure tragedy following the death of a child. Not the most optimistic topic for a presentation but something I thought I was able to speak on for five minutes, and exactly five minutes. A second over time is a costly mistake in Mr Simons' class.

'Okay,' I choke out from the front of the class.

My throat is clear; my vocals warmed and ready to rage through my presentation. But the faces arranged before me fail to demonstrate even the slightest interest in my presentation. A pack of slumped adolescents hang from their seats and ignore their growing sweat patches as well as me. Half the group gaze out the windows into the corridor outside, which itself is not exactly riveting but apparently more interesting than me. Only Mark is making an effort at polite interest, and I can tell that amount of effort is costing him.

The thought of acceptance tickles the back of my mind, never far from my thoughts recently. Would it be enough to find social acceptance with a large group and then use the pack mentality to barge or bargain my way into heaven? *Look at all the people who support me, Jesus. You and St Peter have to let me in now. They're all your children and they clearly accept me and so should you. If you don't, too bad. We outnumber you by quite a few. Your parlor tricks of changing water into wine aren't going to scare us into submission. You're the one who has to change your public view.*

Mr Simons coughs noticeably next to me. I don't know how long I've been standing in front of the class enjoying my inner monologue, but apparently he's the only one who has noticed that I haven't said anything relevant to the topic. A fly buzzing around Randal's head appears to amuse most of them. I know I wouldn't be the first in the class to freeze on the spot during a presentation. At least I'm not on the verge of wetting myself, which was one incident that did get everyone's attention.

I clear my throat again and look down at the notes in my hand. *These won't do,* I think to myself. I won't gain social acceptance by reading something about a depressed man who wrote sonnets. There's only one option I have and I don't leave myself any time to stop and talk myself out of it.

'When I was looking through the works of Shakespeare, it bothered me a little that so many of his plays were tragedies, and it bothered me even more that the tragedies were, in one way or another, of the characters' own making. And the more I read into it the more I began to see similarities not in the literature he influenced, but in my own life. And it scares me, that if things don't change, than one day my life could become a Shakespearean tragedy too. So the assignment I've prepared for today's presentation is not what I'm going to talk about, but instead I'd like to speak to you about something much more personal and meaningful.' I pause for effect, and let my speech cards fall to the floor for added emphasis, but I still don't gain any particular focus from anyone in the room. All right then, here goes.

'I'm gay.'

I wait.

I hear a pencil snap in the sudden silence. Bodies turn rigid in their sunken positions in the seat. A chill fills the room. Mr Simons gapes wide, a fish gasping for air. An uncomfortable shifting shuffles through the room. Mr Simons raises a finger to interject. I hold out my palm to him. *I've already gone and done it*, it seems to say to him, *damn well don't interrupt me now.*

'Now I think that's grabbed your full attention. You all know me, you know who I am. I've studied alongside of you in this school for at least three years now, and with some of you for a lot longer than that. I've prayed in chapel with you, played sport—admittedly badly— with some of you, gone camping with others, and even smoked cigarettes with a couple of you. And for the most part these have been rewarding experiences for me. But there's a part of myself that I've always kept secret, hidden, for fear of what might happen if others found out. But Jesus has always taught us not to fear, and I can tell you firsthand that this fear is a killer. I don't want this fear to be my tragedy. And so I stand before you all to face that fear, to speak aloud that secret, and to tell you that I am gay.'

As the various brains before me confirm their ears have heard correctly, and yes I did just come out to an entire English class, the disbelief on their faces transforms into a range of expression: shock, confusion, even anger and disgust. Mark's expression of pride and apprehension is a beacon for me, signalling a bizarre clash of emotions, a pretty close reflection of my own. I know he's impressed that I've been brave enough to take this step in high school, but also worried for me and what it may mean for the rest of my time here.

I begin my rant. I cover everything, well not my encounters with Thomas—that's his story. He's the one who has to share that information when he's ready.

'The first obstacle in all of this has been actually admitting to myself that I'm gay,' I declare. 'Sure, you can think of it as a simple case of whether you like guys or girls but it wasn't that easy. I want a family, I don't want to disappoint my faith or community and I always thought I would do just that if I were gay. Being gay, I've always been taught, was wrong. I'm sure many of you think that right now. How can I possibly be normal if I'd want to have sex with a guy? That's not how people reproduce so how can it be natural? For ages I thought it wasn't natural, that it wasn't in God's design, yet here I am. I feel these things and in my mind I feel perfectly normal, at least I think I do anyway. Then I started to think if God is a perfect being then how can he be wrong in creating me the way I am?'

My rant is fluid, flowing effortlessly in a stream of baffling contradictions. Everything I say I dismiss or approve through my own patterns of thought. Five minutes doesn't cover it. I rant and rant and rant, covering the first discovery of my sexuality, the denial, the confirmation and beyond into the seemingly impossible waltz of religion and un-straightness. Baffled stares mingle with nods from my peers. A timer beeps and is dismissed instantly, my tale evoking a greater level of concentration than anything on the topic of Shakespeare.

'Everything I feel, everything I believe is part of who I am,' I affirm. 'I can't be expected to change that for anyone. I'm gay. Plain and simple. It's not a struggle to understand, it's not rocket science, well, not anymore. I'm gay. This was how I was born. Take it or leave it.'

By the end of my declaration, my soul is laid bare before this assembly of my peers, open to be trampled or tended as they will. But to my surprise I'm not fearful. Instead I feel lighter, unburdened, and I wonder if this is what confession is supposed to feel like—surrendering the guilt and fear and shame to something beyond myself, where they are swallowed up in the void.

The siren signals the end of the lesson period, and that

I'd just spent the better part of fifteen minutes talking. The two remaining speakers would not get their turn in front of the class, though I sense no disappointment there. But even though both the class and my rant have ended, there is no movement, no gathering of books in preparation to leave, merely silence. I can't move either, caught in their gaze, waiting for the judgment to fall. As the seconds pass, my unease grows and fear starts to creep its way back in. I close my eyes as the dread builds to ward off the retribution I'm now sure will follow.

Instead I hear a tentative clap echo through the room. A second follows, and a third and fourth. Quickly the room bellows with the sound of applause. I open my eyes to the sight of my classmates standing to applaud me. They're applauding my difference, my decision to carry it openly. They're applauding their acceptance. Now more than ever before do I believe there's nothing wrong in whom I am, and they're applauding to show their faith that this is how I'm supposed to be.

When I open my eyes again I see there is one dissenter. Chris refuses to stand and accept me as a peer, his glare hot and hateful. He sulks with arms folded on the edge of the crowd, but his bigotry makes him the outcast here. His presence quickly fades from my awareness along with the doubt and uncertainty in the face of the overwhelming demonstration of acceptance.

Mr Simons pats me on the back, spurring on my pride. I'm too engulfed in the success of my presentation to notice is it not the most encouraging of pats.

'I would usually send you to see the principal,' he whispers gently to me. 'But in this case I suggest you go straight to the student counsellor.' He speaks up to the rest of the class, who are still applauding the occasion. 'Sit down everyone. The presentation is over.' He whispers back to me, 'get your stuff and head on to Father Donovan's office. And I'll expect your presentation on Shakespeare next class.'

I follow the instruction, unsure if I'm in trouble or not, and completely uninterested anyway. My feet skip me along quickly to Father Donovan's office. I beam a tremendous smile of success as I bounce into his office.

'Sounds like you've had fun,' Father Donovan says neutrally upon my arrival as he places the phone on the receiver. 'Mr Simons called ahead to tell me what happened in class. Honestly, I'm proud of you. You've shown a lot of courage to discuss what most would suppress out of fear.'

I sit down, still shining and ignorant of his twitching eye.

'I think we have to talk about this a little,' Father Donovan continues. 'This is a huge step, not only for you but for the school. What happens next is going to impact on quite a few people. News like this will travel fast, and I have no doubt that the principal will be on his way here to speak to you very soon.'

'Wait, what? Why?' I deflate a little.

'The school is likely to take a different view of today's events than you or I, or even your classmates. The principal will be concerned that the school's image might be threatened, or some nonsense like that. Don't worry. I'll be right here to support you. We'll get through this yet.'

'But what does the school's image have to do with me?'

Father Donovan stares at me blankly. I match his stare, dumbfounded by any implication in his look. Gears click into place and throw up the obvious answer: this is a Catholic school.

'Something like this might reflect badly in the eyes of some parents and the school might not be able to condone any behavior that's outside of the church's official teachings,' he says.

I sink silently into the seat, thumbs twiddling before the unknown onslaught from the principal as he stalks into the room. Father Peter isn't the most liked person in the school; his focus is too strongly on the punishment of sinners and ensuring their repentance prior to entering the gates of heaven. Well, that's the impression he gives when he enters the room: there's nothing about a loving God. Look at Him twice and He'll smite you down, now here's a ruler over the knuckles for thinking dirty thoughts. I wish this was exaggerated, but unfortunately that's how Father Peter comes across—old-fashioned and spiteful. It's not long before the door belts open, the power of Christ compelling it to bang against the wall.

'Right, we need to talk,' Father Peter seethes through his teeth.

He stares right through me, eyes glowing red from rage, or hatred, or due to the warming temperature. I can't be sure and I'm not brave enough to ask. His frail frame holds him higher than pride, eating is apparently a luxury from the looks of him. The thinness of meagre nutrition even extends to the grey hair on his head.

'It might be better if we keep this conversation a little private,' Father Donovan suggests, nodding towards the open door.

'Very well,' Father Peter hisses, slamming the door shut and creaking his way to the seat next to me. The stench of old man seeps into my skin, my pores, and most distressingly, my nose, which begins to drown in the foul odour. 'I hear you made a declaration to your class about you being a—' he chokes on the word, glowering down at me, ready to spit in my face, '—homosexual,' the word a sour taste lingering on his tongue.

I nod, more a shiver than a definite head movement.

'That's a very serious misconception and misunderstanding of yourself and your faith,' Father Peter growls.

'How so, Father?' Father Donovan questions, his voice neutral and calming.

'Homosexuality is a terrible sin and cannot be tolerated in this school.' Chills whip my spine. Can I really be booted out of school for something I thought God chose for me?

'This is a fine Catholic school that I'm running. We're able to direct boys toward the correct life in line with our faith and homosexuals do *not* follow that correct line. We can assist anyone away from homosexuality but we both know well the tale of Sodom and Gomorrah.'

'Ah yes, and now the term "sodomy" has been adopted to describe any form of immoral sex.' A glint flickers in Father Donovan's eyes. He appears amused by the situation, knowing this debate all too well, and pleased at of Father Peter's squirm at the mention of anything sexual. 'And as we both know those cities were destroyed because of their immoral practices that were against the will of God.'

'Exactly, homosexuality is against the will of God.'

'Not exactly, Father.'

'Excuse me. The Bible quite clearly states that a man must never lie with a man as a man lies with a woman.'

'Oh yes, that would be clear upon any cursory reading of the text.'

'My understanding of the Bible is a thorough one, I can assure you. How else would I be allowed to run such a school?'

I can't believe what I'm witnessing; to challenge Father Peter is unheard of. I could not have even imagined it might happen behind the scenes, and definitely never expected to witness it from this uncomfortable wooden chair. From my previous discussions with Father Donovan I can guess at the direction he's heading, but encumbered by his rigid adherence to dogma, Father Peter could have no idea that it's a trap!

'I'm glad to hear that, Father. A thorough scholarly reading would reveal to you that the Bible does not at any point mention homosexuality as a sin,' Father Donovan asserts.

'Excuse me Father Donovan; I do believe you are mistaken.'

'Actually Father Peter, I am correct in this matter,' Father Donovan enforces.

Father Peter's face sags in disbelief, dragged downward by an unrelenting force of gravity. I doubt anyone has ever challenged him with such conviction. Father Donovan continues. 'The passage you quoted is from Leviticus, and in the Hebrew text of that particular verse explains that the sanctity of a woman's bed that must not be defiled, and to turn the faithful away from the practices of other religions. The Bible states the sins of Sodom were rape and adultery, and the genders of those involved in the rape and adultery are not important. Gomorrah was destroyed for its sins of greed and lack of charity, and again no mention homosexuality. The use of the word sodomite in the Bible refers exclusively to Canaanite priests who engaged in fertility rituals in the worship of their heathen god, and is thus a condemnation of idolatry, not homosexuality.'

'You speak out of place, Father. You speak against our Lord.'

'No, I'm just accurately interpreting what has been written about His laws in our Bible, and the scriptures it is derived from.' Father Peter gapes impotently, fury boiling inside his eyes.

'Our Holy Father would never condone any form of homosexuality in a Catholic school. We must not allow any form of homosexuality in this school,' he spits, his neck wobbling furiously.

'Actually, the Pope's teachings of Catholic law will and must change. Otherwise we'd still be teaching that the Earth is flat and the centre of the universe. The Catholic church must embrace all loving pairings. In our own Bible the covenant of love between Naomi and Ruth, two women, is endorsed and celebrated before God as a blessed union.'

'But… but… it's immoral.'

'That may be the direction of your own moral compass, but it is not the teaching of the Bible. The Bible preaches love above all else, and through that we must embrace all our students and our wider community, whether you personally support it or not.'

'As the principal of this school I have every right to suspend or expel students if they choose to violate Catholic teachings.'

'Actually, you do not. If you suspend him based on a declaration of homosexuality you are breaking several of our school's policies. All of us are sinners, and to single out one just because you don't like that particular sin is morally reprehensible, particularly as there is no scriptural basis for that sin. And school policy is ultimately set and enforced by a committee of parents and teachers, and I guarantee that I hold more sway there than you do. Should you decide to take this further, then I will write to the Archbishop recommending a review of your position. Any form of discrimination against anyone will not be tolerated in this school.'

'Don't make threats that you cannot follow through, Donovan.'

'This is not a threat,' Father Donovan continues evenly. 'I completed my theological studies under the Archbishop, as you should know. He shares my understanding. We are not here to judge what our Lord would or would not approve of. We're here to guide our students through life's choices, forgive their misguided behaviours and accept the differences that God has blessed them with. Any action of yours to the contrary would see you knocked down quite a few rungs on the ladder. I would hate to see your years of hard work crumble due to a misguided and discriminatory act.'

'I have every right to dismiss a student from my school and the same goes for teachers,' the invective of Father Peter's words is as visible as the catapulted spittle.

'Yes you do, when there is just cause, which right now you don't have. But you can try it in this case if you want. It will make for interesting conversation when I have dinner with the Archbishop tonight. As you know, we remain close friends and he just happens to be in town tonight.'

Defeat and malice twist Father Peter's face into a grotesque mask. I didn't believe a religious figure could explode from such pure hatred towards another person. Father Donovan has the trump card and there's nothing Father Peter can do about it. I'm not sure what this means for my remaining years at school, but at least I'll be allowed to stay.

'Very well,' Father Peter hisses. 'But you're responsible for the actions of the boy. Anything that happens in the school because of him will rest on your shoulders. Mark my words.'

'No Father, you're responsible as much as I am to ensure that the Catholic values of love and forgiveness are practiced within the sentiment of this school, and in the light of the courageous and forthright actions of this student today, and I believe this offers an unprecedented opportunity to address the school to encourage these values.'

One final glare down at me and the rickety old man shuffles out of the room, murmuring bile upon his exit.

'Thank you,' I stutter out after he leaves.

'Don't worry about it,' Father Donovan answers, unfased by the whole confrontation.

'You really stood up for me.'

'Not just you. I stood up for my own beliefs.'

'But no one ever does that. I don't think anyone has confronted Father Peter like that ever.'

'They usually don't, but this is something I'm passionate about, and it also helps to have friends in high places.'

'Is it true what you said about Sodom and Gomorrah? About it not condemning homosexuals?'

'Yes. Everything I just said is true. When you study the ancient scriptures that the Bible it compiled from, there's nothing that speaks against consensual sexual or romantic relations between members of the same sex. But over time the Bible has been translated and revised many times, and sometimes passages are mistranslated, or words are substituted as there isn't a corresponding word in the second language, or some are even deliberate changes influenced by public sentiment against homosexuality at the time. And people with their own prejudices will misrepresent passages to serve their own agendas, or many perhaps haven't even read it and just believe what they are told.'

I ponder over this new information. All this time the answers were right in front of me and I was looking at it from the wrong direction, that I'm different and that difference is wrong. I had always known I needed my own acceptance, but never thought that the Bible would accept me too.

'So me being gay is not against the Bible?'

'Not at all.'

'It isn't a sin?'

'No, according to original Word of God, there's no sin in being gay. There's nothing wrong with being who you are. But there are many out there who believe it is, and will use their own understandings of the Bible, or anything else for that matter, to justify their bigotry, to hide that their beliefs are nothing but hate.'

'So I can be gay and Catholic?'

'Of course you can be, if that's what you choose. I think you can merge those two parts of your identity quite easily. The difficulties you will face are with others, like Father Peter, who aren't able to reconcile the apparent conflict so easily. They will seek to ridicule you, strike you down, convert you, change everything about you to ease their own discomfort, so you will have to remain stronger in your faith, and in your sexuality, than most people are required to when they are challenged by what life throws at them. And the best and most difficult challenge you will face is to forgive. You have to be able to accept everyone for who they are and forgive them for it, and accept the Grace of the Lord to help you to do it.'

Forgiveness. It doesn't sound too hard, until I think of Chris, and the attacks and the humiliation I've suffered at his hands. Confronted with those memories I don't want to forgive, I don't want to let go of so many things that Chris and other arseholes have done that are hateful and violent, as though I don't have it in me to let go of something that has caused me so much pain. But there's something else in Father Donovan's words, something I've heard so often that it barely registers anymore. The Grace of God isn't just a phrase though. It's a real source of strength and peace that I can draw upon to face these challenges, to use when confronted by these people and I have to forgive them, even in the face of their rage and discrimination.

'Thank you for your help,' I say as I turn back to Father Donovan. 'Why did you stand up for me?'

He shrugs. 'It's my job and I really do care about the wellbeing of the boys of this school. We are responsible for the type of men they become,' his eye twitches, 'and I can understand a lot more about difference and forgiveness than most men of the cloth. I've seen and lived a lot in my travels.' The right eye twitches again.

'Oh, okay. Well thank you. I'd best be off to class.'

'Okay, but be careful. You're going to get a lot of questions from the other boys about what you've told them. Are you sure you're ready for it? If not we can arrange something else for you for the next few days, just until the news of your speech dies down a little.'

'No, I think I should be alright. I feel like I've been ready for this for a while. All the different questions and answers have run through my mind at least a thousand times.'

'Very well. But if something happens, or you have a run in with one of the students or teachers, feel free to come to me and we can have it sorted out quickly. This school doesn't tolerate any form of discrimination despite what Father Peter says. There are policies in place to protect all students and teachers, and we take pride in our anti-discrimination approach.'

'Thank you again. I think I should be off now.'

XI.

STRESS AND SINS

JESUS did die for our sins, this I know. And so to not sin a little every now and again would be a bit of a waste. I mean the price has already been paid, and it would seem almost ungrateful to not get full value out of it. Sin and forgiveness aren't about living as puritans to avoid sinning, but there to set us free, so that we can live as we want to, and then be forgiven for any sins that might happen in the meantime. So I'm not sure why I'm worrying about sins right now. Talking to Father Donovan last month helped me get over the fear that I'm a sinful person by nature, but now we've reached exams and I would be a little relieved if a dash of sin snuck into my life and distracted me from the stress and the pressure.

Gossip and rumours about my speech reverberated off the walls of the school for a week or so and then it quickly became old news. I was surprised at how fast it did. The school must be more modern than I thought. Except for some teachers, the ones who never had an issue with me but then looked at me like a poor maimed creature struggling for life and them not knowing what to do to help. They flinch on the spot, unsure if they should approach or let nature takes its course. At a distance they were able to ensure that they didn't catch anything from me. Who knows, one whiff of my cough and they could catch the gay, or so I laugh to myself. I don't think anyone else is prepared to take humour in the situation yet. I'm probably the first openly gay person a lot of them have had to deal with.

Even the usual bullies don't know what to do. Gay bashing always appeared as a central part of their professed machismo, but confronted with me they're baffled. They look at me in confusion, wondering if hitting a gay is like hitting a girl, before they decide it's not worth the risk and wander off to bash their heads against a tree or whatever it is meatheads do to occupy themselves.

One marked change was the drop in perving opportunities in the change room. Before coming out, guys in the change room were completely unselfconscious of their bodies, but now I feel like I'm kept under a careful watch. Rather than strut and crow like before, they act subdued and dress quickly, unsure of how they should be around me as if I were some intruder. Mark keeps a careful eye on me too, and hovers closer than usual. I worry that some guys will assume he's my lover but he's more worried that I'll be bullied. He's now even more my bodyguard and best friend. I'm not sure if he's paranoid and nothing is going to happen, or if the risk of confronting Mark in the process of getting to me is keeping me safe, but no one has come near me the entire time.

Their paranoia in the change rooms has been easing for the past week with the threatening spectre of exams taking over our timetables. The biology exam currently before me is the perfect tool for honing the imagination.

The real test is to manage the boredom, to focus on the questions rather than let my mind wander from dull pages to a more exciting land of my own fantasy. Ah, what a gay land it is, but not a useful one for me to answer all these questions in time. I shake my head clear of distracting thoughts. That must be the real challenge of exams, to keep focused on the blur of questions sprawled out before me. I force my eyes down onto each individual question and demand a response from somewhere in the depths of my brain.

Somehow, I'm still not sure of the exact nature of it, but I manage to fill in all the answers, and leave it up to fate as to how I go. Fate meaning the generosity and mood of the exam moderators and their convictions as to whether or not I should be rewarded with repeating the same year level. I realise this sounds melodramatic, but biology is the one subject where I fear this is a real possibility, and one I can never allow. I've just been through the process of coming out and passing through the novelty stage of being the school's gay. There's no way I want to repeat that process again in a new year level, nor the inevitable confrontation between Father Peter and Father Donovan. There's enough tension caught up in that relationship to snap the bones of anyone caught up in the midst of it. Rather than get caught up in this scary possibility, I turn my attention towards the prospect of freedom for the summer after just one more exam. Freedom to work many wonderful hours in a coffee shop that is bound to run out of coffee at least once. I never thought it would be possible for a shop to run out of its core product yet my manager continues to prove me wrong. It isn't enjoyable to tell customers we don't have coffee, but as long as I'm still paid my work in the café will continue.

I meander peacefully down the ramp that leads out of the examination room, blurs of biological diagrams and scrawls of ink still whirling through my head. So much so that I'm caught by surprise when a rough hand grabs my ribs and throws me to one side.

'Out of my way, faggot,' a voice growls behind me.

My head collides with the side of the building, sending my vision reeling and my reflexes dazed with pain. I'm too stunned to react, and can only listen to what goes on around me.

'What the fuck was that for, Chris?' another voice whirls past me.

'Yeah, what's your problem Clapham?' a third chimes into the mix.

I grasp onto the railing to prevent myself falling completely face first into the wooden ramp, only dimly aware of what's going on around me. Scuffling breaks out at the end of the ramp. The commotion is a mere hum in the background of my swelling head. My brain pulsates against my skull, threatening to burst at any moment.

'You're such a prick, Chris,' Randal spits. I'm a little surprised by his presence on my side of the argument.

'So what? He's a faggot. Are you a faggot with him as well?' Chris taunts.

'You know it doesn't work like that, Chris,' Mark chimes in. 'If you had half a brain you'd know what this is about.'

'I know that everyone who supports him is a poof,' Chris grunts.

The numbers close in on Chris. My vision clears to see he's alone, circled by a ring of my classmates. And while few among them match Chris' strength, the sheer number of them counteracts any muscle Chris can flex.

'What the fuck is this?' Chris tries to maintain his dominance through a failing voice. 'You're all fudge-packers now?'

'No, we just think you're an idiot, and beating up on someone for no reason makes you a massive tool,' Roger adds.

'Fuck you all then,' Chris flicks his hand at everyone and retreats out of harm's way.

The guys watch as Chris withdraws, then return to chatting and wandering back to their classes as if nothing happened. Mark ambles back to me where I'm still clinging to the rail.

'You okay?' he asks.

'Yeah, I think I'll live. My head is killing me though. Thanks for standing up for me like that. And to the others as well.'

'I don't think you have to mention it. Chris is a bastard.'

'Yeah, but I didn't think there would be many at school who would stand up for me because I'm gay.' My chest wells with gratitude when I think of how many guys had been willing to stand up for me.

'I don't think your sexuality had anything to do with it. No one likes it when Chris acts like that. No one really likes Chris much at all, for that matter. We're not about to let one of our own be victimised like that. School can suck enough without people like Chris.'

'I guess. But what I meant was I didn't think that anybody would stand up for me. Because I'm gay.'

'Well, there's always me,' countered Mark, looking a little hurt.

'Of course there's you, that's a given,' I reassure him. 'I just thought that people would turn against me, or think I'd deserved it or brought it upon myself, or worry that if they defended me or associated with me, then their sexuality would be called into question too.'

'Like I said, this really isn't about you,' Mark repeats. 'We all know what Chris is like, and none of us want to be on the receiving end of his bullshit. Sure, Chris might have decided that you're his target this week, but that doesn't protect anyone else. We all have to go through high school and its lessons together, and whether you think you're different or not, those differences don't stop you from being one of us. And I'm sure that we will continue to show Chris that we won't stand for him messing with one of us.'

I nod. It must be true. Everyone gathered around and stood up not for me, but against Chris. Mark was the only one to actually check on me afterwards, to make sure I wasn't bleeding too much. Everyone else left when Chris did.

'Come on,' Mark pats me on the back. 'Time to go to class.'

'Why? It's not like we'd be able to think straight just after an exam and what's just happened.'

'I know, but we aren't allowed off campus.'

'Why not? None of the teachers are going to force us to do too much in class anyway. They're happy enough to be left alone so they can start working on our report cards.'

'What do you propose instead?'

My mind flutters for a moment. I hadn't even expected Mark to consider the idea of cutting class, but now that he's indicated he might consider it, I need some time to think of what we might actually do. The ache down the side of my face doesn't help my concentration, but an idea occurs to me. I allow myself a sly grin and offer an option that Mark, surprisingly, seems to take to instantly.

* * *

We make it to the shopping mall without any difficulties. Mark offers none of the resistance I might have expected from him, and if the bus driver had any concerns about two students apparently skipping school he didn't share them with us. Shop assistants too must be used to students still in uniform roaming the mall when they should be in class. At this time of year there might be a few year twelve students shopping about who don't have classes anymore, just the thrill of exams.

'I can't believe we're doing this,' Mark says as we enter the sports store.

'I can't believe you're doing this.'

'Huh?'

'You're too much of a clean cut student and role model sports player to cut classes to go shopping.'

'You're right, I usually wouldn't, and I think this might be my last time too. The guilt is killing me.'

'Don't worry about that too much. We're already here. Going back to school now would only get us caught.'

'I guess so, and besides, we've been working hard this year. It would be nice to spend a little bit of the money we've earned.'

'Exactly, and I get to flex my gay muscles for the first time.' Mark shoots me a glare with a sly smirk. 'Not that muscle. You know that one has been used already.'

'Yep, and a couple of times,' he teases.

'Could be more than that.'

Mark throws his hands up in defeat. 'I don't want to know,' he says.

'Fair enough. What I was actually referring to was fashion sense. I don't want to define myself by a stereotype, but at the same time while I do know that I'm gay I don't know how to *be* gay. So until I can find some kind of role model to teach me, I'll just have to work it out for myself, and the first step is to find out whether I have any kind of awareness of fashion.'

Mark laughs and leads us through the basketball section of the store. For a straight man he has an odd obsession with balls. Any size, any shape. As long as they fall under the category of balls (and sport) he's happy. They don't even have to be the bouncing type, just balls.

However, sports stores are not where acceptable fashion is to be found, and eventually I'm able to peel Mark away and on to today's challenge, the designer shops. Jeans, shirts, shorts, everything you could possibly need to look fabulous is sprawled across countless racks, causing an effect that is a little overwhelming, but I'm determined. Choosing one at random, I eye over the shop's contents ready to stake my claims in the store. I'm going to find something fabulous and fashionable at a fantastic price, and I just hope that there's some natural gay instinct to help me to do it.

I soon find out there isn't. My taste in clothing is horrid. I can't coordinate colors, I can't tell the difference between daring and tacky, and the outfits I put together would be more suited to a couch from the seventies or one of those people who enjoy dressing their pets up in shameful costumes. And what's worse, I don't even enjoy it. Boredom rapidly takes hold. I completely fail to be excited by the possibility of what I might find, and I'm much more interested in the possibility of getting out of the store as soon as possible. I'm a little devastated, though also a little encouraged that at some point a homewares store caught my eye as I rushed to escape one of the clothing outlets. Perhaps there I will be able to salvage some skill and pleasure in shopping, and hopefully that will count towards some gay points too. I grasp desperately to that hope, as otherwise my humiliation will be complete, given Mark's unexpected flair and interest in fashion.

My only previous experience at shopping with a straight man has been with my father, which usually involves trips to the hardware store to stare at planks of wood and screws and other such nonsense for three hours. The only other image of the straight man shopping that I know of is the boyfriend bored stupid while his girl tries on shoes, or something. But Mark whips shirts and jeans of the rack in a precise fury. He can somehow see exactly what works together and how to choose the right size without so much as glancing over the labels. The sales attendants seem to adore him, while I just fade into the background.

Mournfully I realise that *I'm* the bored boyfriend as I stare numbly at the door to Mark's change room. I'm so bored that I'm vitally interested in the stain that countless handprints have made on the painted white door. The smears dance together to alter their shape according to the angle of view. I hear Mark jabber away in the background about some bargain pants he's found.

'They must be getting in early for Christmas,' he hums with pride. 'Either that or they're clearing out their shelves ready for new stock. They must need the room for them to get rid of such great jeans so cheap. I'd pay double for something like this.'

I'm baffled and very jealous. I feel cheated—it never bothered me that Mark excelled so much at sport, but shopping, *for clothes*, is supposed to be a gay thing. My thing. He isn't even gay. Has he somehow absorbed my gay powers and left me with none like X-Men's Rogue. I'm left brooding in envy while my best, *straight* friend uses his wonderful sense of fashion to find himself a bargain for the current season. I can only tell that this is what's happening from the running commentary Mark considerately provides me from the change room. Every now and then he opens the door to parade a spectacular selection that fits him and his wallet perfectly. I give a neutral compliment, and die a little inside. Mark tries to help me too, offering a shirt he claims will compliment my eyes, but I decline to try it on, not willing to do anything that would prolong the torture.

'Shit,' Mark whispers, from inside the change room.

'What? Did you realise that shirt is from three seasons ago?' I'm glad to see my snarky gay power is still intact.

'No, I'm snagged.'

'Huh? How did you manage that putting on pants? Scratch that, I don't want to know.' Not anymore anyway. A few months ago it would have been a different scenario.

'Not that. It's the tags. There's so many of them and now they're tangled and I'm stuck.'

'Is that even possible?'

'Apparently. Can you come in here?'

'What? No way. I'm good out here, thank you.'

'Please. I need help.'

'What about the shop assistant? It's their job.'

'Just get in here and help. I don't want to look like an idiot in front of them.'

I comply reluctantly and slide into the change room with Mark. I've seen Mark topless many times before, but the change room offers only a very tight space, and the sudden close proximity to his chiseled torso is intimidating. Small tufts of hair poke out from his nipples and sprout upwards from his exposed briefs, but the rest of him is smooth, and the tight bulges and crevices honed by his endless sporting endeavours prove to be a nerve-wracking distraction.

I shake my mind free to focus on the task at hand. Mark is definitely tangled, so much so that I can't work out how it was possible. He could have panicked a little and made it worse, but the complex twists of tags and material has formed some kind of Gordian Knot. The shirt Mark had been trying on hangs limply from its tag, which is entangled with the tag from the belt (selected instinctively from a vast range), the bargain jeans, and somehow… another top. The four tags hold all the clothing and one of his arms together at the back of the jeans. Mark would have been spinning like a dog chasing his tail as he attempted to free himself. I snicker a little to myself—I might not be the most successful gay in the world, but at least I can put on pants without assistance—and start to feel a little better about the whole gay instincts thing.

I get to work, concentrating on the tags, not the fact I'm at eye level with his sculpted butt and playing with his pants. Five minutes or more pass before the beast is freed. Mark sighs his relief while I organise his selections on their appropriate hangers to avoid the whole thing happening all over again. I spin around, finding myself nose to nose with Mark, who was watching me over my shoulder, not that he had any other place to watch from in the tiny change room.

'Cheers,' he says.

'You're welcome. Um… this is awkwardly close.'

'Yeah, um… I've just had a thought… um. Can I try…?' he asks. I'm baffled by what he means. Try what?

'I'm not sure I…'

'Can I try… kissing you?' Mark interrupts me.

My heart launches into a barrage of palpitations. The earlier numbness returns, not from boredom this time, but from panic. I cannot move. I cannot speak.

Mark must be able to read this from my widened eyes. 'I'm just curious,' he continues. 'I'm pretty sure I'm straight. I'm attracted to girls and all but I just wonder what it's like. And not just what it's like to kiss a girl, but also what it would be like to kiss another guy. And because you're gay, and my best friend and all, I just thought you might want to. Um… that's not offensive at all, is it?'

'It's only okay because it's you,' I assure him. 'But I'm not sure what to say.' Internally I know. I had wanted this for such a long time, but now when he wants it I don't. It took a lot of looking at myself to get to the point where I was comfortable with being friends and nothing more, and I didn't really want to risk that now.

'It's just a kiss. And it's better that I learn from some-one who knows what they're doing.'

'I haven't done it that much.'

'More than me. And besides, I don't want it to be some random guy who goes blabbing about it. We know where we stand as friends, this is just one friend, helping the other out with no extra attachments or repayments required.'

'Oh no, you're gonna owe me. But, I guess so,' I break out through the nerves.

Mark steps closer still, pressing his chest firmly against mine, and leans forward without a second thought. He clearly wants to do this. I can smell the sweetness of his breath and feel the heat that radiates from his lips as they seek out mine. I lean into the kiss, fear and excitement twisting a tango in my stomach. Our lips connect. For a moment neither of us moves, freezing in the heat of the moment. I sense Mark wants me to take the lead in this dance, and I like the idea of taking the active role with someone I'd always seen as so masculine. I tenderly part my lips, encouraging him to do the same with my tongue. Mark responds to direc-tion, and sucks me in for a more passionate embrace, his tongue massaging mine.

The fear subsides, boredom rises quickly from the depths. Mark is a terrible kisser. All those nights spent dreaming about intimacy with Mark was just that: dreams. No sparks fly, no endorphin-fuelled connec-tion flourishes between us. A little bit of moisture passes between the tongues but that's about all the exchange offers. We slowly pull apart. My wide open eyes spot a pensive Mark contemplating the situation behind closed eyelids. I wait, tempted to tap my foot impatiently.

'Nope,' Mark mutters after a minute. He opens his eyes to stare honestly at me. 'Does nothing for me.'

'Me neither,' I mumble, 'I'm going to wait outside now.'

And that's exactly what I do. I wait outside the shop for Mark to make his purchase which, after all the combinations he tried, was a single pair of jeans. I let him carry his own bag. I fantasise momentarily that he's my minion to carry all the important fashion purchases and other shopping I'm attending to.

'Thank you for doing that,' Mark mumbles as we stroll aimlessly through the mall. He doesn't look at me while he speaks.

'No worries,' I answer. 'So this is something we don't tell anyone about?'

'Exactly. Just between us.'

'Good, good. Not something to write home about,' I can't quite keep the grin from my lips.

'What's that supposed to mean? Was I that terrible?'

'Well, you weren't that fantastic. There weren't any fireworks going off or anything like that.'

'Is it because I'm straight?' Another question that baffles me. I image any other guy from school would be angry at the criticism of him performance. Not Mark, he just wants to understand.

'I don't think it has anything to do with sexuality. The more I learn I find there is very little it has direct impact on. My guess here is that it would be more about compatibility than orientation.'

'That's interesting.'

'How so? You have kissed girls, haven't you?' I ask.

'Yeah, I've kissed a few.'

'But…?'

'But, they weren't that good. It didn't do that much for me, and now that kissing a guy didn't really work out either, I think maybe it's just me. Like I'm the problem.'

'That is interesting. You might just not be a very sexual person.'

'Possibly. I don't have any problems when it comes to beating off, but I guess I haven't really opened myself up to other people doing it yet,' Mark mindlessly overshares.

'So, you haven't tried sex with anyone else then?'

'No,' Mark answers candidly. 'I've been in a situation when it could have happened but nothing did. I didn't want it to. I'm starting to think I don't have a sexuality.'

'Surely you would have a sexuality. You just can't define it yet. Don't think that just because you're straight that you have any less to figure out in that department than I do. At the risk of encouraging you to overshare again, what do you think about when you're taking care of things, y'know, by yourself?'

Shame washes over Mark's face. He looks around furtively, as though he's about to share a closely held secret. He leans in to whisper out of the hearing of passersby.

'Sport,' he says.

'What!?'

'Sport. I think about sport when I, you know, wank.'

'Now that's definitely interesting.' I resist the urge to chuckle in the face of Mark's embarrassment. 'Can I ask why?'

'I don't know,' he shrugs. 'I guess, well it's just, when I play sport my heart takes off. The adrenaline, the speed of the game, knowing every muscle in my body has to work and pump at some point, it all excites me. And the satisfaction of being exhausted and winning fairly is just so exhilarating for me, I love feeling it and the relief at the end of it.' He hangs his head a little.

'It's nothing to be ashamed about. Just think about it. I'm into guys. Some guys at schools are into girls and no doubt there's one who likes both or just themselves. We're all different. What we're into is different; everyone gets off to different things.'

'I guess you're right,' a little bit of hope rises in Mark. 'I just have to find what does it for me.' We continue to walk in silence for a couple of minutes, vaguely taking in the contents of the windows we pass. 'Why did you agree to kiss me?' Mark asks after a while.

I shrug. 'When in Rome, I guess.'

'What's that supposed to mean? You're that easy, are you?'

I punch him on the arm, the butchest thump that I can muster. It's more effective than I thought it would be. Mark yelps and rubs his arm.

'I am not a slut,' I say. 'But I think I'm willing to explore and experiment for a while, no matter how much others might consider that to be a sin. I accept now that there's nothing wrong with my sexuality, that's not what will ultimately determine the person I will be or how I'll be judged. And if it is a sin, well Jesus knows we can't live without sinning, which is why he sacrificed himself, so that there could be forgiveness. And it's sinning that allows us to forgive, and that's the real challenge in life.'

'That's deep,' Mark ponders for a moment. 'You've had way too much time to think about that. How do you have time to study when you think all the time about sex and sin,' he laughs.

'Not all the time,' I smirk. 'Just most of it.'

'So, what sort of sins are you thinking of doing?'

'I don't think you can handle knowledge like that.' We laugh for a few seconds, thinking about the possibilities of all the sins in the world.

'Actually, I'm curious now,' Mark considers. 'What sort of sins are you thinking of doing? Not drugs or anything like that?'

'No, no way would I take drugs. We've had the consequences drummed into us for years, all the damage that they can cause. I don't want any of that, not even cigarettes.'

'What about more sexual adventures?'

'No, not straight away. I'll wait until I'm ready. I wouldn't mind going clubbing and trying out things in the gay scene. It's just something I haven't tried yet.'

'Yeah, but that's not really something to be forgiven for.'

'True. So should we try midget racing, then?'

'Huh? Jockey racing? We could just go to the horses.'

'No, actual jockey racing. Not jockeys on horseback, just the jockeys themselves running around,' I explain.

'You're joking right? That wouldn't exist.'

'Yes I'm joking. I'm more into dwarf tossing, anyway.'

Mark just rolls his eyes. 'What about cheating or something like that?'

'Cheating at school.'

'Yeah, you could steal the answers, sell them. That would probably require some serious forgiveness.'

I think on it for a second. As far as sins go, it's not exactly exciting. It might make a little bit of cash but it doesn't have quite the same thrill as sneaking out for sex.

I spot something out of the corner of my eye. My heart stops. I grab Mark's arm to force him to freeze on the spot.

'What is it?' he asks. I nod in the direction of a familiar man.

Mark follows my gaze to Father Donovan, and we jump instantly behind a pillar.

'What's he doing here?'

I shrug in response. I thought Father Donovan would have to be at school all the time as well. Mark peeks from behind the pillar for a better look.

'I think the guys on the footy team might be right about Father D being a creep.'

With all that Father Donovan has done for me, I don't like that word being used to describe him, and it's all the more shocking coming from Mark. But Mark wouldn't speak like that carelessly, so I glance out also to see what's going on. Father Donovan is easy to spot in his black robes. The colourful bag from some confectionary store in his hand bulges almost suspiciously, as he browses through clothing on a rack. Slowly, our mental cogwheels spin into place and the penny drops. Mark gasps out loud, signaling that he's spotted it too. Father Donovan is looking through clothing in the *women's* section. And he isn't just browsing—even from a distance we can see his face light up in excitement as he rifles through the selection of bras.

'Let's go,' Mark suggests. I don't argue and we take off back the way we came, intending to catch the first bus that leaves the mall. Not necessarily the first bus back to school, just anything to get us out of here. 'Why was he looking at women's clothing?' Mark asks the obvious question.

'Maybe it's his fetish,' I theories 'I read that dressing up in women's clothes is a relatively common fetish for men.'

'But didn't you say that fetishes are sexual things?' Mark argues. 'Are priests even allowed to have sex?'

'Well, Father D is pretty unconventional for a priest. I doubt he follows all the rules.'

'And did you see that huge bag of candy?' Mark exclaims in a panicked voice. 'What if he's gonna use this fetish thing on kids? We have to tell someone about it. We can't let something like this go. Everyone says he's a pedo.'

'No, everyone who listens to Chris says he's a pedo,' I try to be the voice of reason. 'And besides, I don't think we can do anything about it. Buying candy and looking at women's clothing aren't exactly criminal offenses. And it would mean telling them we wagged class, which I can't be bothered explaining. It's just not worth it without any hard proof against Father Donovan.' I picture going to Father Peter with this news, but immediately dismiss it. Even though I know he'd hate being in the same room with a confessed homosexual, and he probably thinks I'm possessed by some kind of demon, I can imagine how much he'd love to use something like this against Father Donovan, whether there's any truth in it or not.

'So what do we do?'

'Nothing. There's nothing we need to do.'

I'm suddenly confronted with the fact that despite all my talk of sinning, the things I've considered doing really don't amount to much. But there are some people out there in the world who do things that are evil. You hear about them on the news, doing things like molesting children. And even if it's not Father Donovan, some of those people have been Catholic priests. I wonder if some sins are just too big to forgive.

We settle a little by the time we reach the bus stop, enough to calmly wait for the correct bus to get us back to school in time to leave again. This is a precision art, the business of cutting classes. I don't know how people can do it all the time. Surely the stress must take its toll on them, constantly checking their watches, guarding their faces from anyone who might recognise them and report their behaviour to the school.

As I sit with my head against the bus window, staring out, I absentmindedly rub my cheek. It hasn't swollen up like I'd thought it might, but without a doubt the headache tomorrow morning will be killer. The bully's mark, I think. It doesn't always show on the outside, but it lingers on the inside. And it's not even the pain that's the worst part. It's the shame and fear, the humiliation, the sense of exclusion, the worthlessness that the bully makes you carry around with you. It waits in your head, tricking you into panic, or makes you spend all your attention looking for the next attack instead of just living your life, or convinces you it's not even worth facing the world today, so you just hide away and withdraw in whatever way you can. But I'm no longer unarmed against it. My heart swells at the memory of my peers, standing up against a homophobic bully. I feel safer to be part of a community that won't tolerate his bigotry, and accepted in that community, my classmates. And now they appear in my mind too, standing off against the shame and fear and humiliation.

XII.

IN SUMMER IT BEGINS, AGAIN

FINALLY, finally… heat! I relish any opportunity to strip down to basically nothing and enjoy the sweet breeze of the electric fan on my skin. I can do that when I'm home alone, and often do. I can't imagine the horror of nudity in front of my parents or sister, though. Handling that fallout is something I don't look forward to. *Yes mother, I'm still your same little boy, it's just that things are a little different down there since you last saw it all ten years ago.* But here at the beach, where stripping down is suddenly socially accepted, and I can enjoy a sweet sea breeze caressing the hairs on my legs as I attempt a tan. Although the Australian sun is more likely to bestow upon me a hellish, tomato-red burn, which once the skin peels away leaves me a dazzling white again anyway. Still, this place is worth the almost hour-long trip in the car with my sister. The water shimmers an endless clear blue, with only a few mild ripples detracting from the stillness of the surface. You can park a kilometre either side of this beach and you'd find yourself on the open ocean, unfriendly waves and lashing sands. This little cove is a perfect haven from discomfort and from unwanted guests. Only the locals who know to travel out of their way come to this place. And us.

Mark and Sarah have both toddled off to enjoy the

coolness of the water, leaving me to relax on a towel two feet too long. Sarah needs some convincing (and nagging) to drive her kid brother and his friend anywhere, but she always manages to have a good time with us once we hit the road. I have a feeling the usual tantrums and subtle squeals are all a show for my parents, or to haggle a better deal out of them. But out here she seems a different person, one who's much easier to get along with. It can't hurt that I offered to do dishes when it's her turn to sweeten the deal. And in this moment, it's definitely worth it. The sun is my companion and the sand my cradle. The feeling of freedom that resonates within me is a powerful rocket fuel, soaring me leagues beyond any normal man's voyage. Up here nothing threatens me and nothing can hinder my flight path. Unless you count gravity, which I've been avoiding for some time now. Crashing back to Earth and burning off my layers upon re-entry is something I don't wish to perform at present. Flying high is my goal, free from school, free from work, and free from the closet and the pressures of religious conformity. I'm especially glad to be free from the closet, and don't intend to go back in, ever. It's a comfortable and warm place that can protect and smother you in a slow compressing embrace. Coming out has lifted the burden of conformity and provides the much needed space to grow. And more space in the closet for clothes, of course. I wonder whether the reason gay men buy so many clothes and stuff their closet to bursting is so that there's no more room for them to ever fit back inside.

A spray of water wakes me from my musings. Mark and Sarah plonk themselves onto the towels either side of me.

'See, a girl can beat you,' Sarah says to Mark with a wink.

'Girls only win against guys when they're racing a gentleman,' Mark chimes back in the most sophisticated tone he can muster.

'Ha, gentleman. There's nothing gentle about what sportsmen do.'

I detect an inkling of flirtation in Sarah's voice. It's not the first time she's seen Mark topless, but I think this time she's realised how much of man he's become. I hadn't considered this possible explanation for her mood. I wonder if I should tell Sarah that Mark's a terrible kisser, but that would be mean, probably more so to Sarah than to Mark. Though I should probably tell her that Mark likely has no idea whatsoever that she's flirting with him. Mark would need a diagram with written instructions, and even then there are no guarantees. Sarah has no chance against Mark's personal choice of a partner: sport.

'So, what are we doing tonight?' Sarah probes. She must be intent on making something happen, she rarely offers to spend more time with us than she has to.

'Well it's a school night,' Mark says, not remembering that school is done for the year. Sarah giggles airily.

'So, isn't that more of a reason to stay out longer?' she says. 'Let's be rebels and stay out past nine o'clock,' she mocks.

'Cool, really? You'll get us home later?'

'Yeah, I won't drink or anything so I can make sure we all get home. So, what do we want to do?'

This over-courteous sister of mine might be something to watch. It could end spectacularly, either from the tremendous fail (amusing) or with my best mate achieving a first-time life experience (uplifting) with my sister (gross). Time will tell, and I'm keen to follow the progress and possibly encourage either spectacular finish. Mark and Sarah continue the conversation by contemplating where we should take the evening. We have to go somewhere new, where no one knows us—Mark and I are both still underage. He'll pass for old enough, while I'll just have to hope I'll pass by association. Otherwise the only other option is some underage hangout, where the young, skinny boys are nothing to write home about.

'What about Scream?' I suggest.

'What, the gay bar?' Sarah wrinkles her nose. I nod.

'There's a gay bar in town?' Mark blinks aimlessly.

'Yeah, it's something I've wanted to check out but never could be bothered with sneaking in,' I say. 'It could be fun, especially on a weeknight. I have a feeling all the shows are on during the week and the parties and drugs and stuff all kick in over the weekend.'

'Sounds safe enough for a weekday,' Sarah adds. 'I've been there on the weekend and that's something I don't want to repeat.'

'What was it like?' I ask, completely unaware of Sarah's previous trip to Scream.

'Loud, a little disgusting. It was on a Saturday night and I think the party drugs had already kicked in. People were basically screwing on the dance floor while still dancing. On the plus side, the music was fantastic and none of the guys were desperately trying to pick us up.'

'What about me?' Mark sighs.

'What about you?' I tease.

'You'll be fine,' Sarah offers. 'You're cute, so only the cute ones will hit on you.' Mark doesn't look eased by this notion. 'Besides I'll be there to protect you.' I swear there were a few flutters of her eyelashes in that moment. Sarah might actually be trying to hit on Mark. This is going to be a better night than I thought. I had anticipated a nice day, relaxing on the beach, no worries to haunt me and now we're going to top it off by watching the certain train wreck of Sarah hitting on Mark.

It's decided. We're off to Scream. We make the trip back to town by way of the mall to grab a few layers of junk food and appropriate shirts before making our way to the other side of the city. We could have gone home for clothes, but then I would have missed out on Sarah repeatedly trying to get Mark back out of his shirt to try on more in front of her. She's had a whole day of him topless, but now she can't seem to get enough. It's almost as if I can hear the oncoming impact of the wreckage. Mark ducks into a change room for every shirt she throws at him, and every time he returns I have to admit there's something more fascinating about his body when it's hidden beneath the fabric.

We ply our stomachs with the greasiest burgers we can find and pile back into the overheating car. One day Sarah will earn enough money to buy a car with air conditioning, until then we're waving our arms around like chicken wings to avoid patches of sweat spoiling our new, cheap shirts. Mark did it again, found the biggest bargain in the store. *There must be a little bit of a gay man in all of us.* I chuckle a little at my double entendre, but don't bother sharing it, because Mark wouldn't get it. My mind does amuse me sometimes, and now gay jokes (the ones for us, not mocking us) are a whole new venture. It's just a pity that I have to keep them to myself, simply because neither Mark nor Sarah knows anything about the gay world. Not that I'm an expert yet, but with each new experience comes a little more enlightenment, and not just about the gay world—I feel I've broadened my horizons of the world in general much more than some of my classmates have. Some may have delved into new and perhaps risky ideas, but the others would have any 'inappropriate' thoughts beaten out of them with the Bible.

It surprises me that only a few months ago that same Bible was the source of my repression, and in that time I'd been through a journey, first rejecting it, then finding a way of embracing it so that it embraced me. Once again it had become a part of my very being, but no longer one that tortured me. Its pages—its words—cement my footing into the foundations of my life. I live how I need to and the Holy Word holds me up. It doesn't reject me—it can't reject, that's not what it's for. The power of

His Word overrides any form of rejection and pumps forgiveness into the veins of the world—it is quite literally a life support. If only people would allow themselves to see His Grace, pulsating in the vibrancy of His Word and His world, they would come to find an understanding of the Bible as I have. I will fall, I will fail, but through all of that I will be me, and I will also be forgiven. And I know I will also succeed, through His Grace and His strength. I'm a gay man and I'm Catholic. I'm confident now that my sexuality is part of God's path for me, and it doesn't matter what anyone else's opinion is. As I settle further into this way of thinking, I find it fuels my happiness, my ability to relax, and gives me confidence to be in the world, and it's these blessings that faith has provided me that I want to be able to share with others in a similar position.

I don't realise that I've spent the entire drive from the shopping centre pondering until Sarah swings around and squeezes her car into an available park a short walk from the nightclub. I'm starting to feel apprehensive about my first visit to a gay venue, and the vista on the street outside of Scream doesn't fill me with hope. The seediness of the area is punctuated by the litter blowing along the ground, the tumbledown buildings, and the men walking along with tattoos covering more of their bodies than their clothes. For the first time ever I'm thankful that my sister drives such a rundown old car that blends in with the surroundings and won't draw attention—I'd hate for it to be stolen and have to walk home through this part of town. I feel a little vulnerable walking along such a rough street towards a known gay club, and perhaps Sarah and Mark feel the same way, as we all seem to huddle close as we sneak our way along. We hear, and feel, the throb of music before we even see the building, hidden up the back of a block. As we get closer, bricks seem to shake from the thumping from the building's heart, the mortar shivering as the walls bulge outwards.

My nerves peak as we near the entrance. I've never snuck into a nightclub before, never done anything even remotely this type of rebelliousness in my tame life as a Catholic schoolboy. I hope my anxiety doesn't show on my face as we walk in, heads held high with an arrogance that hopefully adds years to our age. Sarah's fine. She's old enough and has her driver's license to prove it. Mark and I on the other hand have only our school cards, and we're not going to start jumping about with them in our hands. I notice Mark shudder slightly in front of me, and I'm kind of glad to see I'm not the only one to feel the worry tickle up and down his spine. But as much as it's nerve-wracking for me, Scream must be an even bigger lion's den for Mark—I'm sure his muscular good looks will make him a very attractive target in a seedy gay bar.

'Excuse me miss,' the bouncer greets us at the entrance. He bulges more than the building and looms like a fortress between us and the door. His all-black attire radiates dominance over any situation. *He knows,* I think to myself. He has to know we're not supposed to be here. 'ID?' he holds out his sausage fingers to Sarah.

She smiles daftly and hands over her license. 'Thank you,' he grunts, handing her card back. 'Have a good night you lot. Two-for-one spirits until eleven and the shows kick off from ten.'

He stands aside to let us past. Relief flushes through me, yet I'm hesitant to completely relax. I'm in new territory. The darkened hallway puts me in mind of a long throat leading into the bowels of the beast, the darkness just an entrance to the heat and damp inside. Here the music is louder, the throbbing more violent, compressing the space around us.

We soon step out into the guts of Scream, and it's almost shockingly clean. Tables are arranged neatly throughout the entire complex and small balcony areas are lined with seats turned to face the stage and catwalk that strike through the centre of the lower level. Twinkling lights and hanging lace and leather dangle suggestively from the ceiling. Two bars face each other off from opposite corners of the club as through preparing for a fight, one overflowing with ice machines and coloured liqueurs, the other sporting a strikingly butch selection of beers and whiskeys.

'You guys grab a seat and I'll fetch us some drinks,' Sarah instructs over the music before heading directly for the cocktail bar, though I'm not sure if that's her taste or if she's just getting into the theme of the night.

Mark and I ease our way through the slowly filling room and take a seat on the left side of the stage, giving us a good view of whatever show is on tonight. We have our backs to one of the balconies so we don't have to watch directly behind our backs for anyone who might spot our age. Sarah returns quickly with six bright drinks in plastic martini glasses clutched precariously in her hands. Awkwardly squatting she manages to get them onto the table without spilling much of their contents.

'Feeling festive are we?' I tease.

'Hell yeah,' she answers. 'Two for one. I thought we may as well get in theme and find as many colours as possible in our drinks.'

'I thought you weren't drinking.'

'I'm not, these are all for you.'

'What?' I gape. 'How are we supposed to get through all of these?'

'I'm sure Mark will be able to get through what you can't,' she winks. Instantly her ploy becomes glaringly clear, and would be for anyone except Mark. I cringe at the idea of my sister getting my best mate tipsy for her own nefarious purposes and sip on the first of the drinks. Sugar rushes in first to soften the sting of the spirits following behind. Mark takes a tentative sip of one as well, shrugs his approval and takes another sip.

'The setup is completely different to last time I was here,' Sarah forces the conversation forward. 'There were no chairs and tables down here. It was all dance floor. The DJ was up on the stage and heaps of near naked people were up dancing on the catwalk.'

'I hope you weren't one of those people,' I shudder.

'I may have been. I had to get out of the sea of sex

on the dance floor. It was the only way to breathe,' she laughs. 'It was a great night when I think about, other than the guys grinding into each other. I don't know why I didn't think of bringing you here earlier.'

'I know why you thought of it now,' I nod in the direction of Mark.

'Shut up,' she says loudly with a playful slap. She leans in quickly once Mark is distracted by the traffic lights that just turned on in the corner of the room. 'Do you think he's interested in me?' Sarah whispers.

'No,' I say, speaking the truth. The smile stays on Sarah's face.

'You're just saying that because he's your friend.'

'Yes, that's exactly why I'm doing it,' I let the sarcasm roll out.

'What show is on tonight?' Mark throws himself into the conversation.

'By the looks of it, drag,' Sarah answers. She apparently has a better knowledge of this place than she lets on. 'That's my guess anyway. I can't think of any other reason why they would set up a stage and tables like this. It has a real cabaret feel to it.'

I let Sarah continue to ramble through her knowledge of gay culture, her words spilling out in a desperate attempt to maintain Mark's attention. The club is filling up quickly. The rush of people flows straight through the entrance hall and splits into two, one stream to each bar. It's soon obvious that there is a clear divide between all the people present. The beer and whiskey draws a crowd of bearded men with hairy chests dressed in tight leather ('Bears,' Sarah informs us). Their counterparts look more like glitter-bomb survivors. They are fabulous in their appearance. Tight, tight (oh so tight) shirts cling to wafer-thin bodies to show off their six-packs. Squeezing in between these two extremes, the leather and frocks, the curious ones venture into the venue. Part of me has the idea that they're family, come to support loved ones during their show. A bit like a Christmas performance at school, only with less clothing and more high heels. How proud would some of the mothers be in here? I would say very, otherwise they wouldn't have come in support. I guess they weren't as strictly controlled in their religious upbringing or their parents were hippies or something. I wonder how proud my mother would be to see me perform in drag.

The lights dim without warning.

'Oh, it's starting,' Sarah nudges me in the arm. 'How does it feel to be amongst your own?'

'Who? You and Mark?'

'No, amongst other gay people?'

'I'm not sure yet. I think I've found a place in myself where I don't have to stress about fitting in with my sexuality but I don't know where I would click in a place like this.'

'That's nice that you're comfortable with yourself. When did that happen? You should've told us.'

'A while back. It's never something we really talk about.'

'Shh,' Mark cuts in, watching intently to see what happens next. We wait a few seconds. The scuffling backstage echoes clearly into the silent room. Some chuckle, apparently knowing who it might be stirring the dust out the back.

'Ladies and gentlemen,' a man bellows through the speakers in a showily flamboyant voice. 'Welcome to the Thursday night of your lives. This is Dragging On, the best, most infamous drag show in town and you're all lucky guests. Just to housekeeping. No phones allowed, unless they're on vibrate (suggestive chuckle) and no screaming orgasms either. Your phones aren't allowed to interfere with our glorious presentation and neither are you; we can arrange a time for that later,' a return chuckle from the audience scatters across room. 'If you need to duck out to suck on a fag the beer garden is out past the two back corners. While you're out there you can have a cigarette as well. And those of you closest to the stage beware, sequins will fly so I recommend glasses or burying your face somewhere, you decide where.' More laughs fill the room as the crowd warms to the salacious commentary. 'Now ladies, gentlemen, and otherwise gendered, strap yourselves in and on for Dragging On. Now give it up for our girls Ms Burly Chassis, Latoya Vibration and Beefcheeks Ragu.'

The crowd roars with excitement. Some people must know who they are. Soon we do as well. The three drag queens have barely minced onto the stage bedecked in their shining dresses before they break into song. Feathers fly with every flick of the wrist. The crowd sings on cue and I smile like I haven't felt myself do in years. We sit enthralled through the number, which is followed by another with only enough time in between to ridicule any hapless watcher who fails to appreciate their glory. We soon observe that moving—or worse, speaking—during the show will result in shreds being torn from your person via spectacularly pithy banter. My cheeks ache with the laughter, and I have no time available for thinking between fits of hysterics that shoot pain through my sides. I notice Mark and Sarah are in a similar state—Mark potentially due to disbelief at what they have to say, and the nerve they have to say it. I know on the football field nasty things get said, but I doubt footballers would have the wicked wit of these ladies. Two of the drag queens slip offstage for another costume change, leaving Beefcheeks Ragu to strut her stuff as a soloist. She has a command over the stage unlike the other two. Her words are not as vicious, yet she ferret seek out hidden intimate secrets from anyone in the crowd through bantering conversation. The first victim is a bear with a bad toupée. She spots the wig and sends shockwaves of laughter through the crowd, decrying the fate of the poor hamster who suffered the misfortune of becoming his hairpiece. Everyone else tries their best to fly (cower) beneath Beefcheeks' radar. But when she finds a new victim, she again manages to expose their secret shame before the crowd, where it's torn to pieces and then somehow carefully reassembled to make the victim feel that their uniqueness is special.

I find myself totally intrigued by the drag queen. There's something about her manner that's both confronting and comforting. And familiar—there's something about the way her eyes dart around the room that makes me think of a teacher watching over a class of unruly boys. And then realisation dawns. Beefcheeks' eye twitches—I know I've seen that involuntary tic before. Suddenly, I gasp with a horror that grips my spine. I claw onto Mark's arm, digging my fingers into his skin.

'What?' he mouths over the music.

My jaw flaps wordlessly as I point hopelessly at Beefcheeks Ragu. I can't communicate yet what I can see in the drag queen, but now that I've seen it I'm baffled that Mark cannot. She waddles comically in her heels over to an oversized handbag waiting at the back of the stage. She bends over, intent on her behind jiggling in the air. The crowd rolls with laughter, Mark along with them as he stops trying to remove my hand to concentrate on the performance. *Oh Mark, if only you knew who's arse you were laughing at.*

'I'd like to tell you a story,' Beefcheeks purrs into the microphone. Guys in the crowd whistle dramatically. 'A little story about someone I once met. A man who put all the sugar I needed into my bowl. He gave me that rush I always needed. He's the Candy Man.' She hoists her bag into the air and rips out a handful of wrapped candies.

Hands from the audience fly up, begging for one of the treats in Vanessa V's hand. She throws the first handful haphazardly into the crowd before launching into her styled rendition of the Candy Man song, each note filled with seduction. My hand tightens on Mark's arm. It's confirmed; I know the man behind the drag queen Beefcheeks Ragu.

'What?' Mark demands a little louder, annoyed by my distraction pulling him from the show.

'Father… Father Donovan,' I stutter out, pointing in the direction of the stage.

'What?' Mark stares between my hand and the performer on stage. Each time he looks back at my hand a small tick is added to the list running through his mind, checking off the characteristics and tell-tale signs. Mark turns, spotting the twitching eye, he turns back again, recalling the bag of candy at the mall, and then again as he remembers Father Donovan looking at women's clothes. With each glance Mark's jaw drops lower and lower. Sarah soon becomes distracted by Mark's motions back and forth to the stage.

'What is it?' she asks, her eyes spotting my hand on Mark's arm. Her eyes glower a little before noting the shock on Mark's face. Jealousy fades instantly to concern.

'Father… Father Donovan,' Mark stutters his explanation as articulately as I did mine.

'Who?'

'One of the priests from school,' I explain. 'He's the student counsellor.'

'What!? And he's performing as a drag queen?' Sarah's face shifts from worry to enthusiasm. 'That's fantastic. I thought priests were supposed to preach, not perform and parade,' she laughs.

'I know. That's what we thought,' I fire back.

'Shh,' a voice hisses behind us.

Mark and I jolt upright and focus on the show at hand. Despite the shock of our revelation, we both don't want to be found out for being in a nightclub underage and drinking alcohol. The show continues, our brains too frozen to appreciate the humor washing over the audience. Each song drones together into one out-of-tune marathon of music. The crowd continues to revel in the dark in the entertainment of the night.

We barely notice the next ninety minutes that cruise by, while the energy from the stage never falters. High pace and extreme commitment is all that's on offer until the finale. Confetti rockets from under the stage and balloons float down from the ceiling to the sway of gravity as the drag queens breathlessly take their bows and stalk off the stage. A low music plays in the background as people begin to shuffle from their seats.

A few songs pass and the lights switch on dramatically, burning the eyes of everyone in the room. They must want everyone out in a hurry, using sudden brightness to force the creatures of the dark out into the shadows of the night. An immovable dumbfounded look is plastered on my face. I imagine it's similar to Mark's: long, pale, lips slightly parted. Sarah breaks through our silence in a fit of laughter.

'I can't believe how surprised you guys are,' she struggles out through her giggling. 'I mean, I probably would be too if it was someone I knew, but this is just hilarious.'

'We saw him with a huge bag of lollies and looking at dresses,' I force out. 'Just—I just—I never thought it would be this.'

'This is just too good,' Sarah continues. 'Nothing like this ever happened at my school. The teachers are all too prudish to do anything like it.'

Her hysterics continue while Mark and I sit their shaking our heads. How could we be so wrong? We had believed that a slight twitch and a bag of candy made a priest a paedophile. We were wrong, it just meant Father Donovan knows more about make-up than he lets on and can kick higher in heels than anyone at school.

The crowd continues to slowly file out, leaving only dedicated barflies buzzing around their preferred corner of the club. Sarah tries to continue a conversation with us, but our internal inquisition of what else we could have got wrong twists a hurricane in our minds. Sarah's giggling halts suddenly. A shadow grows behind us, towering over top of us. My breath stalls with the thought of a bouncer hovering above us. I fight the instinct to look over my shoulder at the looming threat coming to throw us out of Scream. But the shadow doesn't move, and I sense it waiting for our next move, perhaps to catch us if we run. I doubt all three of us could rush out fast enough. Mark maybe, but either Sarah or I would have to sacrifice ourselves to allow the others to escape. I turn and raise my eyes, adjusting to the flickering light reflected off the wall of sequins in front of me. Father Donovan stands a metre from the table, shock and desperation gluing him to the spot, his heels digging deep into the cement. His quivering bottom lip indicates his distress at coming face to face with his students, or anyone who might recognise him, for that matter. He still bears a layer of sweaty makeup and an optimistically stuffed bra, but the opulent red wig he wore during the show has been replaced by a more refined, flowing affair.

'I, um, guess I have some explaining to do,' Father Donovan says through a shaking voice.

'No, that's perfectly fine,' I try to reassure him. 'You don't need to explain anything if you don't want to.'

'No I must explain this, so that there are no misconceptions about what I do here,' his voice returns to the usual teacher like confidence, the sort that arrives automatically when a student is present. He knows what he's about to speak about and our role is to listen and understand. He slides a chair over to join us at the table. A gentle wave of body odour sneaks out from his dress. He did really work it on stage. 'I'm sure you have some questions about what I'm doing up on stage here,' he begins.

'No, you go first,' Sarah jumps in, her humour and interest in the situation rising.

'Well thank you,' Father Donovan holds out a hand.

'Sarah, I'm his sister,' she says excitedly, taking his hand and shaking it.

'I've never had to explain this before,' Father Donovan

ponders for a moment. His thoughts align and he begins his explanation. 'You see, I've always been a performer and loved the excitement of getting up on stage in front of a large crowd. I found it one of the best ways to connect to more people and spread a message. I used to perform in anything the school was doing, but once I finished my studies the possibilities were limited. I tried community drama groups and choirs but none of that provided the thrill that I needed. Then one day I went to drama group and there was a poster on the wall calling for drag performers. I was interested of course and thought why not? And now I'm a regular.'

'This is your Thursday night activity?' I begin the questioning.

'Yes.'

'You're a drag queen?'

'I prefer performer and artist.'

'Yeah, but in drag.'

'Are you gay?' Mark chimes in.

'No,' Father Donovan leans in closer. 'I'm a Catholic priest,' he whispers before sitting up straight again. 'This means I'm celibate, and always have been.'

'We saw you carrying heaps of candy in the mall. We thought you were a paedophile,' I cut to the chase without a second thought, the baffling situation enough to block off my personal censorship mechanisms.

Father Donovan laughs. 'I guess that would be an easy conclusion to jump to, with all the stories of Catholic priests and child molestations and cover-ups on the news.'

'Is this why you stood up for me against Father Peter?'

'Yes and no. I know what it feels like to be isolated from my beliefs because I have a passion for something outside the church. But I mainly stood up for you because Father Peter was wrong and a bully. You can't prevent someone from finding their place within a faith or a school based on one individual characteristic. That's not what my understanding of the Bible is and I stood up for it.' Father Donovan shifts uncomfortably. 'I can't stay for very long but, just quickly, can you guys please keep this to yourselves? This isn't something I want to be common knowledge at school. I do love what I do and once students leave the school I'm more than happy to show off my talents on stage, but I don't want anyone at school to have leverage over me because of this.' He pauses, hoping his spiel is enough to prevent us blabbing to the first person we see from school.

'Yeah, we won't tell anyone,' Mark and I say. We wait for a moment before I jab Sarah in the ribs.

'Yeah, yeah fine, I won't tell anyone,' she mutters disappointedly.

'Thank you so much for understanding. I have to go. It was very nice to meet you Sarah and I'll see you lads at school next year. Behave over summer and less sneaking into clubs while you're underage.'

Father Donovan's heels don't hinder him as he makes his quick escape from the club. This wasn't exactly how I thought the night would go, yet here we are. Sarah's so distracted by the missed opportunity for gossip that she's forgotten to make her move on Mark, who's now a little lubricated with alcohol. Mark and I await instructions before Sarah begins to usher us out and back to the car. A crinkling sound accompanies Mark as he stands. Bemused by the sound he quickly pats himself down to find an extra bulge in his jeans pocket. Sarah stares with her continued amusement as Mark pulls out scraps of paper and business cards one-by-one with the private numbers of suitors jotted next to their names.

'But—how?' Mark stutters. Sarah's hysterical laughter kicks in at the sheer amount of phone numbers as she leads us out to the car.

I stare blankly out the window on the ride home, the blurring lights of town ignored by my deepening thoughts. How could I misjudge someone so much, especially after coming through a year in which unfair judgment is exactly what I've personally been confronted with? I'm different and I vocalised it, yet the instant I see difference myself, I jumped to assuming the worst in other people. There's nothing bad in what I do as a gay person, yet it was all too easy for me to assume immorality in another's actions. Father Donovan was never a terrible person to me. He has only ever stood up for me. Guilt steadies itself on my back ready to take another ride. My mind travels over the mistakes I made in labelling Father Donovan as a paedophile and retraces all the words he ever said to me. The task of forgiveness meanders through my mind. That's what Father Donovan assured me Catholicism is really about. This must be my first real challenge with forgiveness: forgiving myself. He only wanted to perform and bring joy to a heap of people, and because I didn't know what he was doing I assumed the worse. Surely forgiveness can't be too hard, but guilt has gained a stranglehold. I shake it off. There's no place for guilt. I need to fight it, to forgive. I shake my mind clear. Forgiveness can only begin once I refuse to concentrate on the guilt and focus on understanding.

It has been a hell of a year. Temptations took me, sexual thrills straddled me, and fear of my true self was left behind through the strength of my friends and family. Change is swift on its wings and it curves around ready to take aim at me for the coming year, although this time I'm ready for it. There's nothing coming in the future I can't handle so long as I understand and remain willing to struggle through the tougher times. I smile and focus on the lights ahead. *I can do it*, I think to myself. *I am me, I am out and I am the man God wants me to be.*

God and the Gays

*The unpublished version of the article that lead to the
creation of Coming Out Catholic*

WE live in a world of sin, or so anyone would be led to believe if they try mingling anything slightly taboo with some forms of religion.

Such difficulties of blending faith with personal identity can be a daily struggle for anyone identifying as both Christian and homosexual.

Selecting quotes from an English religious text without any form of context can fuel the personal conflicts.

Just take the example of "if a man lies with a man as one lies with a woman, both of them have done what is detestable" and you are focusing on a grim outlook for same-sex attracted person holding to these words without background information.

Senior Pastor of the Glory Tabernacle Christian Center in California Sandra Turnbull, who has studied religious scriptures in depth, explained that some extracts without context are seen as "clobber passages".

She stressed further that the term "homosexual" was only coined in 1869 by Hungarian physician Karoly Maria Benkert.

"The term was never used by English Bible translators until 1946," Ms Turnbull said, underlining that lacking these basic details have led to the shortfall in church acceptance of homosexuality.

"Many have argued that the Sodom and Gomorrah story in Genesis 19 was the beginning of God's wrath against homosexuals because of the destruction of these cities," she continued.

"However, in Luke 10:10–12 we see Jesus speaking of Sodom and Gomorrah in terms of the sin of inhospitality.

"Therefore, we should probably take the words of Jesus to heart and understand that Genesis 19 has nothing to do with human sexuality and certainly not homosexuality."

According to Ms Turnbull this story was also never initially seen as a condemnation of homosexuality by the Hebrew people.

That was until approximately 200 B.C. to 100 A.D. when the damaging interpretations began to surface in Jewish writings.

"In much of these writings, when the sexual activities of the people of Sodom and Gomorrah are addressed, the Jewish writers seem to condemn excesses that are both heterosexual and homosexual in nature," she said.

In further discussion with Ms Turnbull she points out two key words that have been translated from Greek and have been considered to condemn homosexuality.

"The first Greek word is 'arsenokoitai' which is… two Greek words put together, the word 'arsen' means man or male and the word 'koite' means bed," she said.

"This word is translated in the New International Version of the Bible as 'homosexual offender' in 1 Corinthians 6:9 and as 'pervert' in 1 Timothy 1:10.

"As you can see by these two translations of the same word, Biblical scholars have struggled to understand the meaning of 'arsenokoitai'.

"The second Greek word is 'malakoi'," she added. "This word is translated in 1 Corinthians 6:9 as 'male prostitute' in the New International Version of the Bible while this same word is translated as 'fine' or 'soft' wherever else it is found in the New Testament."

Understanding the use of these words and verses does not end with the definitions but rather requires an advanced look into the pagan religious rites of the Egyptians and the Canaanites.

"The worship practices of these fertility cult religions demanded the offering of seed or semen to the god or goddess in order to receive the blessing," Ms Turnbull said.

"The priest or prostitute at the pagan temple would receive the 'seed' in the form often of sexual intercourse.

"Thus, the prohibition for Hebrew males in Leviticus 18:22 and 20:13 to have sexual encounters with a 'male as with a woman' is God's way of saying, do not go and offer your seed to these priests and prostitutes."

Looking into the religious scriptures it can be felt that the main themes of the "clobber passages" have been overlooked and resulted in homosexuality being condemned.

"I see that the 'clobber passages' are all linked by the issue of idolatry," Ms Turnbull added.

"The very word 'To`ebah' or 'abomination' in the Hebrew text that has caused so much confusion and condemnation of homosexuals for many years is in fact a word that makes clear only that God hates idolatry."

Ms Turnbull went further to suggest it's not a good theology to apply the ancient texts to modern day homosexuals.

"Many gays and lesbians today are Christians and love Christ Jesus as their personal Savior yet, they have been ostracized from the Church at large because of the misuse of these scriptural passages.

"Furthermore, the human sciences and social sciences also inform us that human sexuality is varied … there is a spectrum of sexuality and so the Church must embrace all of God's creation.

"To err on only emphasizing their sexuality and forget the spiritual component of their lives is a tragedy and not God's purpose at all."

Formerly ordained Queensland Anglican deacon Greg Strutt knows personally the burden of guilt placed upon some people as they develop the belief that their sexuality is not compatible with their faith.

"What I find in my own situation I can get bogged down in the stresses and the problems within the Christian denominations but the thing that is really important to me is living the authentic life," Mr Strutt expressed thoughtfully.

"Some Christians get caught up in the conservative group of people…that's when LGBT people can feel excluded."

Mr Strutt emphasised the dangers of using scriptures out of context and noted: "There's not always an easy answer when some people read scriptures.

"I think it's much more valuable to look to the central teachings of Jesus of Nazareth and what he had to say and how he acted toward people and for me that's a loving acceptance of people for who they are."

Speaking on a personal level Mr Strutt discovered "coming out" to close friends and family was overwhelmingly loving and accepting.

The hurdles and potential mistreatment were usually found in the hierarchy of the churches.

"There have been a lot of people who have unsurprisingly walked away from the church or walked away from faith as being part of their lives after being treated that way," Mr Strutt said.

Hearing the stories of rejection and actually being part of them are two things Mr Strutt has become familiar with although over the years the struggle with conflicting interests has changed very little, especially for younger people raised in a strict religious family.

One young, same-sex attracted woman, Hannah, grew up in this situation and at 20-years-old is overcoming the constant struggle of balancing her lesbian relationship and faith.

"I had been bought up my whole life to believe in

Christianity and that homosexuality is wrong these people aren't going to heaven," Hannah explained.

"I felt like I couldn't talk to anyone because all my friends are Christians… I almost felt like killing myself but then I realised God doesn't want me to feel like this, surely there's a reason for these feelings and then I started to accept it.

"I started to be more confident and then I met my partner and I realised she's a Christian too and I asked her how does she deal with her faith and her sexuality and she said it is a struggle for her as well.'

Finding complete acceptance does not come simply from finding someone who accepts all of you and shares your faith, such as in Hannah's situation which is an ongoing one full of joys and of complications.

"I guess it is kind of hard when I see my dad because he tries to give me the conversion… I always feel horrible coming back from that," she said.

"It is hard to integrate yourself into a church when they don't want homosexuals to be a part of teaching… we are thinking of going to a different church that is actually accepting of gays."

Finding a total balance with a faith and with a homosexual partner is further complicated with the ideals of marriage encroaching into federal laws.

There are those who consider God to cherish any form of love and wish to see it validated in legal marriage and, of course, there are others who see gay marriage as one of the greatest evils.

Even with the current restrictions in the marriage act same-sex attracted people are still discussing marriage for themselves.

"We would like get to married and have a house of our own," Hannah said.

"I see marriage as standing in front of the people you love in your life and saying how much you love the person standing next to you and you want to do life together and you are also saying it in front of God."

Ms Turnbull also notes the idea of same-sex union where "the story of Jonathan and David in 1 Samuel and the story of Ruth and Naomi in Ruth are same gender love stories where covenants are formed between persons of the same sex and love is shared.

"God is a God who has created human kind to be diverse and, as David the psalmist said in Psalm 139, God has formed us in the womb of our mothers and we are wonderfully and fearfully made."

Also by Alex Dunkin:

HOMEBODY

∾

Visit the author's website:
WWW.ALEXDUNKIN.COM